ALSO BY CAROLYN ARNOLD

Detective Madison Knight

Ties That Bind
Justified
Sacrifice
Found Innocent
Just Cause
Deadly Impulse
In the Line of Duty

Power Struggle
Shades of Justic
What We Bury
Girl on the Run
Her Dark Grave
Musrder at the lake
Life Sentence

Brandon Fisher FBI

Eleven
Silent Graves
The Defenseless
Blue Baby
Violated

Remnants
On the Count of Three
Past Deeds
One More Kill

Detective Amanda Steele

The Little Grave
Stolen Daughters
The Silent Witness
Black Orchid Girls
Her Frozen Cry

Last Seen Alive
Her Final Breath
Taken Girls
Her Last Words

Sara and Sean Cozy Mystery

Bowled Over Americano　　*Wedding Bells Brew Murder*

Matthew Connor Adventure

City of Gold
The Secret of the Lost Pharaoh

The Legend of Gasparilla and His Treasure

Standalone

Assassination of a Dignitary
Midlife Psychic

WEDDING BELLS BREW MURDER

A SARA AND SEAN COZY MYSTERY

CAROLYN ARNOLD

HIBBERT & STILES
PUBLISHING INC.

Published by Hibbert & Stiles Publishing Inc. 2023

hspubinc.com

Paperback ISBN: 978-1-989706-92-3
eBook ISBN: 978-1-989706-91-6

WEDDING BELLS BREW MURDER

Chapter One

Sara Cain must have been crazy to set her wedding date only six months out—even when money was no object. It was hard to believe the big day was only one sleep away. Though time did fly. Even more so since Sean McKinley inherited a vast fortune and proposed to her. From there, it was all a blur. They'd quit their jobs as homicide detectives with the Albany Police Department and spent the time since traveling the world. It had turned out Sean's benefactor, Old Man Quinn, was a wealthy businessman with thirty-three companies around the globe—of which they'd visited only a handful so far.

They had returned from Spain a week ago to ensure all the wedding preparations were on schedule. Between a professional wedding planner and good friends who lived in the area, all was covered. Tomorrow was on track to be a perfect day. Fingers crossed it stayed that way.

Ever since Sean's windfall had hit the news, he and Sara had gained notoriety in the press. Reporters from all over the country clamored for an exclusive. Mere acquaintances came forward and claimed close friendships. Sara found adjusting to the limelight difficult, although traveling had sheltered them from some of the impact. But now that protective bubble was gone. They were back on their home turf. More specifically, her hometown.

Cotton Spring Falls, fifteen minutes outside of Albany, New York, came with a modest population of about sixteen thousand. Tonight, Sara and Sean were seated with their wedding party—short their master of ceremonies, who needed to bow out for a professional obligation—in a private room near the back of the most popular mom-and-pop restaurant in town. They'd rented the establishment for the night to ensure their privacy. A small price to pay.

In attendance on Sean's side were his aunt Gwen Dixon, his long-time best friend, Conrad Cooley, and Jimmy Voigt. He was her and Sean's former sergeant and was standing up as Sean's best man. Jimmy had been a mentor to Sean and a bit of a father figure. Sean had lost his biological father at seventeen to a heart attack—sudden, unexpected, and devastating.

Sara had her two closest friends, Valerie Morgan and Bobbi Rowe—both dubbed maids of honor, as choosing between them would have been impossible. Both were single and self-proclaimed to be happy that way, but the thriving businesses they each owned in Cotton Spring Falls kept them busy. Sara's parents, Jeannie and Leon Cain, were also there. They'd adopted Sara as a baby, but they might as well be her flesh and blood. She didn't remember her biological father, who had died before she could form memories, and her mother had run off prior to that. Private investigators had never discovered her whereabouts. It wasn't even certain if she was still alive.

"To Sara and Sean." Jeannie lifted her champagne glass in a toast, and everyone joined in.

"Thank you, Mom." Sara would squeeze her hand, but she was a few chairs down, seated next to Leon at the end of the table.

Servers set out the main course—meals that had been preselected before today by each person present. The food wasn't regular fare offered by the establishment, which traditionally served pub food.

Their dishes set in front of them were salmon with a creamy dill sauce served with grilled asparagus and risotto; beef tenderloin, roasted baby carrots, and braised potatoes; and the vegetarian option for Valerie, which was butternut squash ravioli made with a cauliflower pasta garnished with crisp strips of basil that had been sauteed in butter and oil.

Sara lifted her fork to dig into her beef and saw Sean watching her. They took each other's hand.

"I love you, Sara Cain." Sean leaned toward her, cupping her cheek in his hand and giving her a kiss on the mouth.

"Ooooh… Speech!" Conrad clinked the handle of his fork against his glass.

Valerie and Bobbi were quick to raise their glasses in support.

Sara smiled at Sean, knowing he didn't love being in the spotlight.

"I'd rather save it for my vows tomorrow," Sean said.

"Aw, that's too adorable," Bobbi cooed. As much as she claimed to love being single, Sara wouldn't be surprised if she was the first of her two best friends to tie the knot.

"At least kiss again," Conrad dared.

"Not a problem there." Sean set the cloth napkin that he'd had on his lap on the table and stood. He held out a hand, and she put hers in his.

They "performed" to hoots and hollers from Conrad and laughter from everyone else. Sean gave Sara a kiss that made her head spin.

Prior to meeting Sean, she was fine being single and lived a complete and full life. But from the moment they made eye contact, something shifted. There was this instant, inexplicable connection to him, as if she'd always known him. At the time, romantic notions had to be set aside, though. They were partners on the job, and mixing business with pleasure could mean the difference between life and death. *Thank Old Man Quinn for everything!*

She ate while watching those she loved and feeling so incredibly blessed. She'd marry the man of her dreams tomorrow and not look back.

The plates were cleared, and dessert would come out in a few minutes.

Sara excused herself and headed to the restroom. She passed the kitchen doors on the way, but she stopped at the sound of a raised voice coming from inside.

It belonged to Darlene Day, the woman who had created their masterpiece of a wedding cake. "Leave me alone! I have told you it's not happening."

Darlene's venomous words had Sara blushing. Though it wasn't like she'd intentionally eavesdropped. It had been unavoidable. There was no verbal response, but shoes tapped against the floor. One set of footsteps was coming toward Sara. She hustled to move.

"Sara?"

She froze, put on a smile, and turned to face Darlene. She was wearing a frilly white apron tied around her ample waist. Her cheeks were a bright red, and strands of gray hair poked out from a loose bun and stood out from the sides of her head.

"Hello." Sara wanted to ask if everything was all right, but it was truly none of her business. And if she did inquire about Darlene's well-being, she'd give herself away.

"You must be getting excited," Darlene said. "How was everyone's meal?" She seemed genuinely interested, even though the concoctions were not her creations. Confections were Darlene's specialty and what made Locally Baked *the* bakery in Cotton Spring Falls and nearby townships. She was here tonight to provide a sampling of the wedding cake on offering for tomorrow.

"Absolutely lovely. And you have no idea how excited. But if you'll excuse me…" She smiled and ducked into the restroom and leaned against the wall. She was feeling like a snoop, but it wasn't like she'd intentionally heard what she had. And, besides, she had no context to know what to make of the words.

Sara took care of her business and returned to her guests.

Darlene entered the room with a tray of cake squares and doled them out. "To give you all a taste of the wedding cake being served tomorrow."

Once she got around to her, Sara thanked Darlene for all her hard work and asked after her eighteen-year-old niece, Trinity. Sara hadn't yet met her, having only heard about her from her mother and things Darlene shared. Trinity had lost her parents in a car accident not long after Sara had moved to Albany, and Darlene was raising her. Earlier in the week, Darlene had spoken proudly of her and said she might be here tonight to help her.

"Trin will be there tomorrow, but you know what girls her age are like. She ran off with her boyfriend."

"Tell her that we missed her."

"Will do." Darlene excused herself and left the room.

After espressos and special coffees, Sara, Sean, and their closest filtered out of the restaurant into the cool March air. Her parents and Sean's aunt were the first people to take off, leaving six loitering in the lot—Sara, Sean, Valerie, Bobbi, Conrad, and Jimmy.

"One minute before we leave," Sean said to Conrad and Jimmy—the three planning an overnight stay at Sean's house. She and Sean hadn't let go of their individual homes yet, but after tonight, they'd be calling Sean's house home—at least until they decided to go house shopping. Travel and wedding plans had taken priority in the last several months.

"You got it." Jimmy smiled at Sara and ambled toward his car with Conrad at his heels.

Valerie and Bobbi picked up on Sean's enclosed request to be left alone with his future bride. "We'll be in the car," Valerie said.

Sara nodded, and once everyone walked away, Sean put his arm around her shoulder and pulled her to him. "I'm going to miss you tonight."

"Me too."

They had agreed, based on custom, to stay apart for the night. It would be tough, as they'd adapted to sharing a bed.

"Just one night," Sean said. "Otherwise, I intend to fall asleep with you every night and wake up with you every morning."

"Not sure that's entirely realistic, but we can give it a go." She winked at him, and he smiled.

Before he left, he kissed her tenderly one last time. She was smiling, her soul lit on fire, happier than she'd ever been in her life, but there was also this knot in her gut.

Wedding day jitters setting in or something else? She couldn't quite place her finger on what was causing the discomfort, but it probably wasn't anything important. All she needed was a good night's sleep. Tomorrow she'd become Mrs. Cain-McKinley. How she loved the sound of that.

Chapter Two

The wedding was being held in Cotton Spring Falls Dutch Community Center—a heritage it came by because Dutch traders founded the town. It was a rather large venue with rooms to facilitate the ceremony, dining, and reception. There were also two fully functioning kitchens, meeting rooms, and spaces designated to accommodate bride and groom.

Since neither she nor her family, nor Sean, were associated with any organized religion, this location seemed an answer to their needs.

Sara was in the bridal suite with her maids of honor and her mother.

"There." Bobbi stepped back, having just finished adjusting the tiara holding Sara's veil. "You're as beautiful as ever."

"Thank you." Sara's gaze flitted past her friend to the standing mirror. Her breath caught at her own reflection. The dress had a heart bodice and followed the curves of her petite frame. She was wearing her mother's pearl necklace, the something borrowed. For something new, pearl teardrop earrings, and for a splash of blue, a tiny dolphin charm on an ankle bracelet.

Sara's mother came up behind her, setting her hands on her shoulders. Sara looked at her mother's face in the mirror.

"Bobbi is right, sweetheart. You are beautiful, but I am so proud of you." Jeannie's voice fractured as she spoke the words, and tears pooled in her eyes.

Sara turned, careful of the train on the dress, and faced her mother.

She was clutching a tissue in her hand, and her chin quivered slightly. "I wish you all the happiness that your father and I have." Her mother reached out for Sara's cheek but stopped short of contact. "Don't want to mess up your makeup."

"Then please stop making me want to cry." Sara felt the hot tears building, but blinked them back and fanned a hand in front of her face. "No, no, no."

Valerie laughed. "You'll be crying before this is all over. We are talking about *you* here."

The fact the groom had been completely off-limits just six months ago didn't help with the enormity of the day. How could she speak her vows, while peering into Sean's eyes, and *not* cry given how far they'd come? "Well, if I'm going to cry, I'd rather it be later." An image flashed in her mind of standing at the podium, holding hands with Sean, and the officiant saying, "Repeat after me." *Gulp…* She could always take the coward's way out and avoid eye contact with Sean altogether.

"Here's a little help to push you past the wedding jitters." Bobbi had four flutes of champagne and gave the first glass to Sara.

The wedding was to start in seven minutes. "Do we have time?"

"You're the bride. You set the schedule. To Sara and Sean." Bobbi raised her glass and made the toast, and the rest of them echoed her sentiment.

The champagne was cold and sharp. A wake-up call.

I am getting married!

Her single life was soon to be over. She'd hold Sean's heart in her hands. What if she ever failed him?

"Oh my…" Sara set the glass down on a nearby table and put a hand over her heart.

"Sweetie?" Her mother rushed over to her. "Are you all right?"

Huge question. Tough to answer. Not that she had any doubt she loved Sean, and commitment didn't scare her at all. Their romance was of the once-in-a-lifetime variety.

"Sara," her mother prompted.

"I will be." She considered gulping back the champagne when a knock on the door stopped her.

"I'll get it." Bobbi hurried over, opened the door a crack, and stuck her head out. "Yes?"

The visitor didn't speak, but the door was pushed open, and Darlene Day stumbled inside. She beelined to Sara, a wild look in her eyes.

"Darlene? What is it?" Sara's sixth sense shot the hairs up on the back of her neck. What would have her baker in her bridal suite minutes before the wedding?

Darlene's eyelids were fluttering, and she was panting.

"Ah, Sara…" Bobbi's face was pale as she pointed at Darlene. "She's… ah… She has a…" She covered her mouth and turned away.

Sara tensed and spotted what Bobbi had been trying to tell her.

Darlene had a knife plunged into her back.

"I'm calling nine-one-one." Her mother rummaged in her purse and pulled out her phone.

"We're getting you help. Just hang in there." Sara was calm, despite every nerve ending in her body screaming someone tried to kill Darlene. The knife didn't get in her back by accident. She couldn't have done it herself. It was Sara's former career as a homicide detective helping her to process all this in a rational manner. She leaned into the flush of adrenaline. She motioned for Valerie to help her guide Darlene to the couch. They perched her on the edge of the cushion. "Who did this to you, Darlene? Do you know?" Sara asked.

Tears were falling down Darlene's cheeks, and she opened her mouth and closed it, gasping like a fish out of water.

"It's okay. Just stay with us. That's the important part." Sara fended off the rush of anger that danced through her veins. Darlene was sixty-something years old. What could she have done to attract a murderer? *And today… Why today?* The thought was minuscule, the guilt immense that it had even come to mind.

"I…" Darlene's voice was weak, and Sara assured her again.

"Help is coming."

"… need someone here right away," her mother was saying into her phone.

Bobbi and Valerie were huddled together in a corner of the room, staring wide-eyed.

"Save your energy, Darlene." Sara pinched her eyes shut for a moment, wishing to heal the poor woman and set back the clock.

"I… I…"

It wasn't long before sirens were approaching the community building.

Sara looked at the clock. She was due to walk down the aisle in five minutes. Her heart sank as her wedding slipped away.

"Someone needs to tell them downstairs that..." Sara swallowed roughly. "The wedding needs to be postponed."

Valerie sniffled and nodded. "I'll take care of it."

"Thank you."

Valerie left, and the door shutting behind her seemed to add an exclamation point to Sara's reality. Her marriage was on hold.

Darlene tapped the back of Sara's hand. "I... Icing." Her eyes rolled back just before her head fell forward.

Darlene Day was dead.

Chapter Three

This couldn't be happening… could *not* have *happened.* It was like a horrid nightmare, except there would be no waking up from this one. What was with people around her being murdered? In the days before her engagement to Sean, it had been a neighbor around the corner from Sara's house. She'd been the one to discover him dead inside his entryway. She'd also taken in his beagle, Magnum, who she and Sean adopted. While they traveled, he'd stayed with Sara's parents, who were very much at risk of getting their own fur baby now that they'd fallen in love with having one around. All these thoughts were ricocheting inside her head, disrupting her peace of mind. Surely, Darlene's murder was coincidental and not a sign that Sara attracted death or was some sort of Pandora's Box.

A knock on the door had her jumping.

"Sara?" It was Sean, and she started toward the door.

Her mother tugged on her arm. "He can't see you in your dress. It's bad luck."

"Too late to prevent that." Sara glanced over her shoulder at Darlene's slumped form.

"Sara?" Sean repeated.

"Sean, just give me a minute." She looked anxiously around the room. Should she change or just answer as she was?

"Please, darling, just open the door," Sean pleaded.

Her chest tightened. She was being foolish. The whole "groom seeing a bride in her dress" thing was nothing but foolish superstition. "I'm coming." She swept past her mother and shrugged out of the way as she tried to stop her again.

Sara opened the door and froze. Sean was quite the sight in his tuxedo. So very handsome, and he was all hers.

His mouth gaped open as he danced his gaze over her dress, her neckline, her lips, and her tiara. He met her eyes. "Sara, you are… breathtaking."

Her cheeks heated, but now wasn't the time to get swept away by his charm. "You shouldn't be seeing me right now, but there's been a murder."

"A murder?" His confused expression looked like a scowl. "Valerie said there was an *incident*."

At that point, Valerie came up behind him, slightly winded. She stopped short, her gaze going from Sara to Sean, back to Sara. The unspoken caution was an easy— and predictable—one to pick up. She was giving Sara grief about showing herself to Sean.

"Everyone's been notified there will be a delay," Valerie said. "Conrad and Jimmy are making sure no one goes anywhere."

Sara nodded, realizing her friend might not even understand the full import of that. Someone in this building was most likely a murderer. She made eye contact with Sean. "You need to make sure of that." She didn't need to say any more. Two years of working as partners in Homicide had made them good at reading each other's minds.

"I will." And he was off.

As she watched him walk away, the rest of Valerie's words sank in. Sara took a deep breath, hating to acknowledge reality. There would be more than a *delay* to the wedding; it would be postponed. The community hall was now a crime scene. Speaking of, so was the bridal suite. "You and Bobbi need to leave this room now. So do I. Paramedics will look at her and confirm death. But there's going to be crime scene investigators, detectives, a medical examiner…"

"Sweetheart, you can't seriously be considering remaining in your wedding gown," her mother said, her voice tender and concerned.

Sara considered, and it wouldn't be ideal, so she'd make a change of wardrobe. "I'll change, if one of you can help me out of this." She could barely bring herself to say the words, and her chin quivered as she did. All the hard work to make this the perfect day—for what? It was a selfish pity party, really, as a woman had lost her life. Besides, how could she get married on the flip side of a murder? It wasn't like she could ignore Darlene's body and carry on like everything was peachy. Was all this a bad omen? Was the universe trying to tell her not to marry Sean? She trembled at the thought.

"I'll help," her mother said, as Bobbi brushed past them into the hall with Valerie.

Sara stepped back and closed the door. Walking across the room, she carefully removed her tiara and veil and gave a wide berth to the couch and Darlene's body. She laid it across the back of a chair near the closet and opened its doors. Inside were the Chanel dress pants and blouse she had worn to the center, but her gaze danced over to the other outfit. To think, just moments ago, she had assumed her next change of clothes would be into the sequined pantsuit she'd be leaving in. Ironically, the sentiment about assumptions seemed apt right now. Along the lines of making plans and God laughing. Well, she wasn't, and neither was anyone else.

"I'm sorry this happened to you," her mother said, staying near the door.

Sara slowly turned, sorrow filling her soul with disappointment, but on any scale, Darlene was the one they needed to feel for. And what would become of her niece, Trinity, with Darlene dead? Sara shook her head. "It's unfortunately where we are. We need to find out who did this to her."

"Sara, by that you mean the local police? Not you, right? You're retired, off the force. You don't need to find anyone."

Did her mother not understand the way she was wired at all? She had an inborn need to get answers, obtain closure, and find justice. "She was murdered at my wedding."

"Yes," her mother dragged out and closed the distance. She put a hand on Sara's shoulder. "And the police will investigate. We all need to clear out and let them do their work."

"Mom, no one can go anywhere. This center is now a crime scene." Sara turned and pointed behind her to indicate the buttons on the dress that trailed up her spine.

Her mother started undoing them. "It doesn't mean you have to investigate."

"How well did you know Darlene?" Sara asked, disregarding her mother's words.

"Enough to know Darlene didn't deserve this. I can't imagine who would have done this to her." Jeannie's voice was even, almost catatonic. She was clearly operating in a state of denial. The shock of the death hadn't fully hit her yet.

"We'll find out."

Jeannie said nothing, but Sara sensed her annoyed energy. She finished with the buttons and touched Sara's shoulder, prompting her to turn around. "*We?* This is a matter for the police—not you and Sean."

Sara was saved from defending her decision again by another knock on the door.

"Paramedics," a man called out.

"One minute." Sara fanned her hands for her mother to hurry. Gown overhead and off, she stepped into her pants and buttoned up her blouse. "Come in." She wiped down the front of herself, straightening the material.

Two medics entered. The older one frowned at the sight of Darlene on the couch.

"Ms. Day, and she's…?" He looked at Sara.

"She passed shortly after we called for you," Sara said.

The younger one checked for a pulse, shook his head, and the older man double-checked.

"She *is* dead," he said.

Sara crossed her arms, biting back a sharp remark. It didn't take a rocket scientist to discern between alive and dead. "Did you know her?"

"Yes, she made the cake for my wedding," the older medic said, his eyes dipping down. "That was years ago now, but her bakery is the go-to in Cotton Spring Falls."

"Hands down," Jeannie said proudly as she finished hanging the wedding dress on its hangers and tucking it into the closet. "We haven't met before, but I'm Jeannie Cain, Sara's mother. Ah, that's Sara."

"Otis Whitaker," the older man said. "This is Brice Franklin."

The younger medic dipped his head, blushed, for reasons Sara didn't understand. "You'll need to call in the police, ma'am."

Sara stiffened. "We will. Thanks."

The two medics turned to leave, but Otis stopped to say, "Sorry about your wedding."

"Thanks." The condolence had reality sinking in deeper. The day she'd been anticipating and planning for six months was ruined. Sara snatched her purse from where it had been on a table and pulled out her phone.

"I'm glad you're seeing reason and leaving this to the police," her mother said.

"I never said anything about leaving it entirely with them."

"Sara Melody Cain."

"Mom, there's no way I'm not going to help out."

"And what makes you think the police will be interested in your help?"

Ryan Doyle, a detective with the Cotton Spring Falls PD, came to mind. She'd had him around her pinkie finger since elementary school. She'd invited him to the wedding, but he'd declined. It might have to do with feelings he had for her, which she never reciprocated. She wasn't taking the moral high ground taking advantage of him, but it was a means to an end. He'd likely let her and Sean be involved in the investigation. "Oh, I'm sure they'll be open to the idea." *Ryan anyway…*

"What do you think Sean will say about this?" Her mother stepped into the hall with Sara.

She closed the door of the suite. "I'm sure he'll agree with me."

"Then you're both crazy, Sara."

"Mom, someone in this building killed Darlene. At our wedding. It doesn't get much more personal for us." It grated on her to think that someone she and Sean had invited was a killer. That burden settled on her shoulders and the back of her neck as she listened to Ryan's line ring.

Chapter Four

Sean was making sure their wedding guests were comfortable and staying put. Paramedics had come and left shortly afterward. There wasn't much they could do beyond confirming death.

"Are you going to make an announcement about what happened?" Conrad leaned in toward Sean. "Don't you think your guests have the right to know?"

Sean shook his head. "The less the better." He scanned the faces of those around him, his gaze dipping over his aunt and others who served with the Albany PD. Why would any of them want Darlene Day dead? They likely hadn't even known her.

Among the throng were the faces of strangers—those who Sara had worked with at the local police department and some of her extended family. He'd have no way of knowing who among them would possess motive.

Sean left his friend to look around more—not even sure what he hoped to find. Jimmy was making the rounds to ensure all the exits were sealed off.

Sean headed toward the staircase that led up to the suites for the bride and groom and stood at the base. He expected to see blood droplets here, but there weren't any. None as he continued up the steps either. This didn't make sense. Darlene's wound would have left trace with her every step. And, surely, someone would have seen her walking around with a knife in her back.

His phone chimed with a text from Sara.

Cotton Spring Falls PD on their way. Is someone we invited a killer?

How did he even begin to answer her question? It seemed so obvious. One of the people from the guest list *was* a murderer. But where to begin looking for a suspect? He'd only met Darlene Day for a tasting. He wasn't from this town, whereas Sara had grown up here, likely knowing all the gossip, scandals, and dynamics. Even from what he could tell, Darlene had been a stalwart of Cotton Spring Falls, and her bakery, Locally Baked, struck him as highly lucrative.

Sean, we need to investigate.

He read Sara's latest text, and he hadn't even responded to her first. Her declaration wasn't a surprise, but they had left law enforcement. This next chapter of their life was supposed to be about living—not death. And certainly not murder. Yet they'd barely flipped the first page, and here they were, faced with that very thing. He wasn't sure how to respond to his fiancée. This discussion might be best face to face.

Sean returned to the main level and gestured for Conrad to come over to the base of the stairs. "Just stay here, please. Don't let anyone pass who isn't with law enforcement. Can you do that?"

"Ah, sure."

There was hesitation in his friend's voice. Sean had known Conrad since elementary school, and he was a radio personality, not involved in any way with murder. His professional life was about pumping the airwaves with rock 'n' roll and the latest in entertainment news. The darkest it got for him was when a celebrity died, and he had to share that with his listeners.

"Sean, what's going on?" Leon, Sara's father, stopped in front of Sean.

He'd guess by the man's obvious confusion that the news of the murder hadn't reached him yet. That likely meant Jeannie was still upstairs with Sara. Sean figured the man might regret asking, but told him, "Come with me." He climbed the stairs ahead of Leon.

They found Sara and Jeannie standing sentinel in the hall outside the bridal suite. It chipped at his heart that she was no longer in her gown but in her street clothes— even as nice as they were, some designer she fancied but could never dream of affording before Quinn's money. If Darlene hadn't been murdered, at this moment, she'd be in her wedding gown, and they'd be exchanging rings and nuptials. The only traces left on her person were the pearl necklace and dangling earrings. He was still in his tux, feeling a little overdressed, but there were more pressing matters.

"The police should be here soon," Sara told him.

"The police?" Leon said, shock coating his tone.

"Darlene was murdered," Jeannie said, stepping up next to her husband.

"Yes, and this entire place is a crime scene. So please be careful what you touch," Sara said.

"Don't we have several police officers downstairs?" He jacked a thumb over his shoulder. "Some are even detectives you worked with at Cotton Spring Falls PD."

"There are a few and my old sergeant—our master of ceremonies, as you know—but I have contacted someone specifically."

"The best they have?" Sean countered.

"He is good at his job, but..." Sara left her statement hanging and bit softly on her bottom lip.

Leon's arm was around his wife's waist. Jeannie turned toward her daughter. "Oh, Sara, don't tell me you called in Ryan?"

"I... I had my reasons." Sara nudged out her chin.

Whatever conversation mother and daughter were having left Sean in the dark. "Either of you want to fill me in on what's going on? Who is Ryan?"

"Me too, please. Just a tiny clue?" This from Leon.

It wasn't missed that no one bothered to explain who this Ryan character was...

Jeannie narrowed her eyes and put her gaze on Sean. "What's going on is Darlene Day was murdered, stabbed in the back, and your future wife stubbornly wants to investigate."

Sara sighed and looked at him.

Sean needed to think through his next words so as not to offend Sara or her mother. *Talk about walking a tightrope...* "I'd like to know who did this to Ms. Day and how it could have happened here." He felt that response was as neutral as Switzerland, but based on the disappearing smile on Sara's face and a growing scowl on Jeannie's, it hadn't been received well.

"As I told Sara, you're not police anymore, and this was to be your day," Jeannie said.

"Things change, Mother."

Sean had never heard her take this tone with Jeannie before. He hadn't heard her speak to anyone this way, come to think of it.

"You got your old job back?" Jeannie countered. "News to me, if that's the case."

"Ladies, ladies, please," Sean said. "Let's keep focused on what matters here. A woman is dead. Murdered."

"How did this happen, Sean?" Sara asked. "We were so diligent about making sure that every guest had to present their invitation upon arrival. We paid a security company to put guards on all the doors. Jimmy ran background checks on them."

These measures were to stonewall the media and paparazzi; never had he considered a killer would slither in. "I will speak with the security guys." He paused, then added, "Did Darlene say anything to you before she died?" His gaze slid to the back of the closed door, his mind conjuring the image he'd stored from earlier of the woman's body on the couch.

Sara nodded. "One word. *Icing*."

"Icing? Nothing about who did this to her?"

"Nope. But I'm guessing there must be something important about the icing..." Sara pinched the drop on her right earring but quickly released it.

"What could be so special about the butter cream frosting?" he asked.

"I have no idea, Sean." Her ensuing eye contact said it all. She was determined to follow this through, alone or with his help. But Sean would go along for two reasons: to please his future bride and because he was intrigued.

What had prompted Darlene Day to say "icing" with her dying breath?

Chapter Five

Sara heard the footsteps bounding up the stairs before she saw that it was Detective Ryan Doyle with a woman at his heels who Sara didn't recognize. She must have joined the CSFPD after Sara left. She was dressed in a lackluster navy pant suit with a badge clipped to her waist and a police-issued Glock nestled in a hip holster.

"Detectives," Sara greeted them.

Ryan perched his hands on his hips and tilted his head toward the woman. "This is my partner, Detective Louise Farmer. Run us through what happened."

All business. He hadn't even taken time to acknowledge anyone else, but Sara responded, "We were in the bridal suite when—"

Ryan held up a hand. "And *we* are?"

"Myself, my mother, and my two maids of honor."

"Their names?" Louise had a notepad and pen in hand, at the ready. A sparkling diamond and wedding band adorned her ring finger. She hadn't shown any reaction to the mention of two maids of honor. Sara guessed she had faced the same pain of choosing between two best friends.

"Valerie Morgan and Bobbi Rowe."

"We'll need to speak with them," Ryan said.

He'd tossed it out so callously, one would swear they were strangers to him. Had he erected a wall to help himself retain objectivity?

Sean stepped closer to Sara and put his arm around her waist, and she sank against him, happy for his presence and support. Ryan's questions were standard, but being on the receiving end was rattling. It probably didn't help that she felt like she and those closest to her were under suspicion.

Ryan's gaze slid briefly to Sean, as if he were seeing him for the first time. The men gave no real reaction to each other, but Sara could feel the static charge between them. And it wasn't her ego misleading her or presenting what wasn't there. Ryan had never relinquished his crush on her, proclaiming his feelings for her at every opportunity. She'd been thoughtless and selfish to call him here. Not her finest hour. She'd just been so focused on who would look the other way if she and Sean poked around—an obvious error in judgment. It didn't look like Ryan was going to let them get away with it.

Ryan's jaw was tight as he prompted Sara to continue running through the afternoon's events.

Sara recounted everything from the moment Darlene Day knocked on the bridal suite door to her last word and final breath.

"Icing?" Ryan's forehead wrinkled, skepticism plain to see in every burrow. "You're sure that's what she said?"

"It is. I heard it too," Jeannie chimed in. Her voice was cool and carried a warning to the detective to watch how he treated Sara. Jeannie was acquainted with Ryan's mother before he had entered the world.

"Mr. and Mrs. Cain." Ryan dipped his head at her in greeting.

Jeannie stiffened and tutted. Sara imagined she had found it rude that he'd failed to acknowledge them before now.

Ryan continued. "As you realize, this is a serious situation, and I cannot afford to be seen as extending liberties just because I know… well, everyone involved."

Sara prickled at the remark. *Involved* struck her as a heavily loaded word, the implication being that one of them—Sean, her mother, her father, her best friends, or herself—had something to do with Darlene's murder. Her cheeks heated. "Ryan, I requested you specifically due to that reason. I also trust you will follow the evidence."

He met her gaze, and in the silent communication, she gathered there was more that he wasn't sharing—the true source of his agitation. "I appreciate your confidence and your words, Sara, and I will. Along that vein, what had Darlene in the bridal suite moments before the wedding?"

Sara anticipated this would be one of the questions she'd need to answer, and her mind only served up one possibility. "Darlene knew that I was a homicide detective, and she probably came to me for help."

"*Was* being the key word," Ryan said. "Surely, she could have roused help downstairs."

"I can't begin to explain her thinking, but she would have been in shock." The latter was a weak defense. The instinct to survive should have had Darlene screaming out for help, not trudging up the stairs to Sara.

"Ma'am, if she wanted help, why not ask for that? Why say 'icing'?" Louise angled her head, her long lashes batting against her high cheekbones.

"Again, I have no idea." Sara was inclined to serve up hypothetical ideas but had a feeling her effort wouldn't be appreciated.

"She was stabbed from behind," Sean interjected. "It's possible that she never saw her attacker."

"And your name, sir?" Ryan asked him.

"Sean McKinley, Sara's fiancé." He tensed, squaring his shoulders, possibly an unconscious physical display of his claim on Sara.

Some color rose in Ryan's cheeks. "How well did you know Darlene Day?" He settled his attention on Sean, and Sara took his arm from around her and squeezed his hand.

"Just met her, at a tasting for the wedding cake. I also saw her last night at the rehearsal dinner."

"I see, so she made the cake?" Ryan drew his gaze to Sara.

"That's why she was here," Sara countered.

"That still doesn't satisfactorily answer why she was in the bridal suite. I will want to talk with both of you in further detail," Ryan said.

"Why would you need to talk to Sean?" Sara blurted out. "Sean wasn't even around when Darlene died."

"Precisely, so where was he?" Ryan turned his gaze on Sean again.

Sara narrowed her eyes. "You surely can't suspect he had anything to do with this."

"I have no opinion on the matter at this point, Ms. Cain." Ryan's use of her maiden name poked her temper.

"Sean hardly knew Darlene, as he just told you. What reason could he possibly have? Not to mention, all this happened minutes before our wedding was scheduled to begin. Sean would have been in the hall waiting for..." *Me...* Sara gulped as heartbreak consumed her.

"Is that where you were?" Ryan asked Sean.

"Of course. That's something you can verify with everyone present."

"You can be sure we will. If you'll excuse us…" Ryan flicked a finger in the air, indicating for Louise to follow him into the suite.

Like he was prompting a dog… "Urgh. How dare that man?" Sara was beyond frustrated and irritated. She prided herself on reading people, and she had trusted that Ryan was mature enough—and professional enough—to put aside the green-eyed monster. It would seem she was wrong. "I'm sorry about this, Sean." She touched his arm.

"His attitude isn't your fault," he assured her.

A spike of guilt stabbed her. She had known how Ryan felt about her but chose to call him anyhow. The guilt of that was eating away at her. She had to do something that would make her feel better and could only think of one thing. "We need to look into Darlene's murder for ourselves, Sean."

"Here we go again." Jeannie huffed and looked at the ceiling in a dramatic display. "Leave it to the police, sweetheart, I beg of you."

"Your mother is right this time," Leon stepped in.

"Hey." Jeannie playfully batted his arm. "What do you mean *this time?*"

Leon smiled, and his attempt at lightening the tension worked. Sara could always count on her father to make an awkward situation less so. Now if only he had a way of turning back the clock.

Chapter Six

They could mill about and wait for the detectives to come out of the room or put time to better use. Sara asked her parents to see to their guests, but her mother didn't move.

"I am going on record as saying you should leave this to Ryan and his partner to handle. They still have their badges."

Their badges… Sara never had second thoughts after quitting her job, but hearing it come back in this way stung. Same as when Ryan pointed it out. Earning that gold shield had been the manifestation of a young girl's aspiration, and it hadn't disappointed. Putting a bad guy behind bars or locking up a killer gave her life purpose. But now she had the opportunity to do something fresh and new with her life. She and Sean had thirty companies around the globe and could be involved as much or as little as they liked. They were responsible for the jobs of countless thousands. It was both daunting and exhilarating. *It also comes with purpose,* she thought.

"Sara, did you hear a word I said?" her mother asked.

"Jeannie, we understand, and we won't get ourselves in too deep," Sean said, stepping in on Sara's behalf.

"I will hold you to that. Now, your guests are probably getting restless, even hungry and thirsty. What do you suggest we do?"

Sara turned to Sean. They had caterers to handle the meal, every guest had selected their preferred course when they returned their RSVPs. The staff were scheduled to start preparation once the wedding service had begun at four. Nibbles and hors d'oeuvres were to be offered after the ceremony and before dinner—that being about now, as it had to be at least five thirty in the evening. Still, it was unlikely the guests were starving, and any who had an appetite would lose it once they found out there was a murder in the building. "Everyone should be fine for now. Though it wouldn't hurt to make sure the catering staff stays on top of keeping the pitchers of water topped up."

"And we could open the bar," Jeannie said. "Some people might find a libation helpful to calm their nerves."

The only one here in need of calming was her mother, as most present didn't know there had been a murder yet. And intoxication would only make matters worse. "I think that should be run by Ryan and his partner, Mother. We'd best not disturb him now."

Jeannie's gaze hit the back of the bridal suite door. "Suppose you're right. What ever happened to that boy? He used to have manners."

"Please, Mom, if you would just assure people all is fine," Sara said, though feeling the hypocrisy at her words. Nothing about the turn of events was fine.

"Should we get everyone in the dining hall, just in case Ryan okays it?"

"Just find a quiet place to wait for instructions. Can you do that, Mom?"

"We can do that." Her father was the one who replied and took his wife's hand. They left, and Jimmy was coming down the hall toward Sara and Sean.

Jimmy frowned when he saw Sara. "I'm so sorry." He hugged her, and she sank into her former sergeant's embrace. Her history with him wasn't as long as Sean's, but some people have a way of snaking quickly into one's heart. Jimmy was one such person. She admired his contrasting qualities—the tough cop and leader tempered with a man who believed the best of people despite years of witnessing evidence to the contrary.

"Not your fault," she said, surprisingly keeping emotion out of her voice.

"Did you make sure no one's leaving?" Sean asked him.

"Yes, sir, I did just as you asked."

"Thanks."

"Don't mention it. Have detectives arrived yet?" Jimmy nudged his head toward the closed bridal suite.

"They're in there." Sara pinched the strand of pearls that still adorned her neck, and it was almost as if she'd touched fire. The jewelry was just another reminder of her ruined wedding. She grieved it *and* Darlene Day. *One killer, two casualties.* A dramatic thought but true.

"Whatever you need me to do…" Jimmy said, leaving the end of the sentence dangling, but the offer of help was clear.

"Well, Mom thinks Sean and I should leave the matter to the police."

"You should." Jimmy served that up point-blank.

"What? I thought you just offered to help?" Sara said.

"I meant regarding guests and the like, keeping people calm, that type of thing." Jimmy regarded them. "You are serious about investigating this."

"I knew Darlene all my life, and she died right beside me, Jimmy. She came to me for help, I know it. I might not have been able to save her, but I do intend to find her justice." *What other explanation can there be for Darlene making her way up to the bridal suite?*

Jimmy pointed at the closed door. "That's a job for the detectives in that room."

"They also have procedure to follow," she replied.

Jimmy smiled and drew a pointed finger between them. "I see what's going on here."

"You do?" Sean looked as puzzled as she felt.

"You got a taste for sleuthing when you looked into that bowler's murder."

That bowler had been Sara's neighbor and Magnum's former owner. And speaking of little Magnum, she could do with burying her fingers in his fur right about now. But he'd still be in the care of Hugh Thornton, who had been tasked to watch him until it was time to fulfill his role as ring bearer. And with everything that happened, who knew when that would be.

"It's not that," Sean responded to Jimmy's accusation, but his defense didn't sound convincing.

If Sara were honest, she'd admit that sleuthing around had been thrilling. She'd been reluctant at first, as it required going behind a fellow detective's back, but it had a good ending. The precautions they took to conceal themselves had been fun between the undercover getups and fake backstories. Even Magnum's nose had played an integral role in catching a killer. And while sleuthing, they didn't have to follow the rules and cut through red tape; they had freedom.

"Here's the thing. When you know someone for a long time," Jimmy began, "you can tell when they are lying to themselves."

Sean held up a hand. "Fine. It was—" He turned to Sara and smiled.

"Fun," she finished, quite sure that was where Sean had been headed.

Sean's eyes widened slightly at her response but sparkled with life. "Guess you could say that."

"Uh-huh. But as your friend and an officer of the law, I must warn you. Watch your step, or they could see you as interfering with an active police investigation. I wouldn't want to see either of you locked up on today of all days."

"Not going to happen." Sean cupped Jimmy's shoulder in a lighthearted gesture, but the sergeant's face was somber.

"I hope for both your sakes that's true. Now, anything you need from me?"

"Could you check on Magnum? Please."

Jimmy's soft spot for the hound wasn't a secret. His body language relaxed, and his voice rose a few notches in his presence. Then there was the myriad of dog treats that often manifested from his pockets.

"For you, the world."

"Thank you."

Jimmy turned to leave and spun around as Albert Needham headed toward them. "Oy," Jimmy groaned.

"Nice to see you too, Sergeant Voigt."

Dryer than some champagnes...

Albert Needham was the main medical examiner for the city of Albany, but due to the small size of Cotton Spring Falls, this jurisdiction fell under his domain too. He got along much better with the dead than the living, and the tension between the ME and Jimmy was tangible. Sara wasn't sure when that animosity had started.

"Yep, I'm sure," Jimmy replied coolly and dipped his head to Sara and Sean. "Ciao." With that, he left.

"The body?" Albert raised his eyebrows at Sean.

"In the bridal suite," he said, pointing a finger toward the door.

"Much obliged." Albert's likability was lacking since most of what he said was riddled with sarcasm. Words that, on the surface, might sound polite held a different meaning when they left his tongue.

"We should get started before we have your old boyfriend breathing down our necks," Sean said and led the way to the staircase.

"Not an old boyfriend. In fact, *never* a boyfriend," she corrected.

"Good to know. My respect for you has risen yet again." He smiled at her.

It must have been the underlying attitude directed at him from Ryan. She hoped having both men under the same roof wasn't going to create too much drama. But Sean had no reason to be jealous. If someone hadn't murdered Darlene Day, she'd have already vowed her life to Sean.

Chapter Seven

Sara and Sean went to the main level, and their guests were dispersed around the center. Some were seated on benches in the hallways, while others stood. Most were chatting in small groups until they noticed them.

Sara's cheeks became hot, knowing that many of the conversations pivoted around her and Sean. She hated the look of pity she read on most of their faces. But it wasn't them who truly deserved it; a poor woman had lost her life.

"Sara? Sean?" A young woman came hurrying over, a man about her age at her side. Someone must have pointed them out to her, as Sara didn't know her. The young woman continued. "I heard a rumor. Is it true that Aunt Dar is…?" She stopped there. Her chin was quivering so hard it made Sara think of clothes dancing on a line in a strong wind.

This must be Trinity. Sara hated that she'd found out through a rumor. What were Ryan and Louise doing? And what a horrible basis for a first meeting. "We are Sara and Sean. I'm assuming you're Trinity Fields?" If they hadn't been traveling in the months leading up to today, it was likely they'd have met her before now.

"Well… can you tell me?"

Sara glanced at Sean for strength. In her career, the victims of murder had been at arm's length. Darlene's death was personal—even more so than Sara's neighbor. Sara had known Darlene her entire life. She *was* Cotton Spring Falls. People thought of the Ole Town Hall, another landmark building in town, and it was Darlene's face that came to mind. She oversaw community volunteers and advocated for the small-town residents that she viewed as extended family.

Sean must have sensed Sara's emotional turmoil and guided her toward a vacant chair, but Trinity would need it more than her.

"Please, sit, Trinity," Sara told her.

Trinity did as she was encouraged. When she and Sean worked in Homicide, it was standard procedure for the recipient to sit when being notified that their loved one had passed. There was far less chance of them fainting and getting hurt. Seated, there was less distance to the floor.

Sara, Sean, and the young man formed a sheltered perimeter around Trinity.

"I'm sorry to say that your aunt Darlene is dead." Sara spoke gently. She had a sentiment at the ready, but it rang shallow in her head. Being sorry for the girl's loss would do nothing to set anything right.

"I don't get it." Trinity bunched up her face. "I saw her not long ago. She wasn't feeling that great but… dead?" She swallowed roughly as if choking on the word. Was it due to the finality of never seeing her aunt again or the aftermath she'd be forced to face?

"When did you see her… exactly?" Sara asked, the detective's hat in place.

"No more than two hours ago." The young man supplied the answer.

"And I apologize, but we should have gotten your name. You are?" Sean asked.

"Austin Palmer, Trinity's friend."

At that, the girl reached out for his hand, their fingers grazing, and she amended his summation of their relationship. "*Boy*friend."

A look at a clock mounted on a nearby wall told Sara it was currently six. Two hours ago, she had been in the bridal suite taking care of the final touches. Never in her wildest imaginings would she have seen Darlene knocking on the door, a knife sticking out of her back. "Where was she, your aunt, when you saw her last?"

"She was in the kitchen fixing the icing on the cake. It got nicked in transport. She wanted it perfect for you guys and was trying to get it all sorted before the ceremony but was cutting it close." Trinity's eyes filled with tears. "Sad about your wedding too."

"Yes, well, don't concern yourself with that," Sara said. "But thank you."

Trinity dabbed at her nose with a tissue.

Darlene had been fixing the icing. Could she have been trying to tell her that? But why? It seemed hardly relevant, considering the knife in her back. If it was, Sara certainly didn't see how. "Your aunt was a special woman. And I'd have expected no less from her. So she was fixing the cake when you left her there?"

"That's right. Me and Austin went ahead of her and got seats for the ceremony."

"And we were about fifteen minutes early, remember?" Austin said to Trinity.

"Right. Yeah, so I left Aunt Dar at about quarter to four."

Sara pieced together the timeline. Darlene had shown up just five minutes before the ceremony was to start. Her killer must have acted within a ten-minute window then, between three forty-five and three fifty-five. Very tight. Almost too tight to be believable. Had the person who stabbed Darlene been present when Trinity saw her aunt? "Was anyone else in the kitchen with her?"

"Not that I saw. You, babe?" Trinity motioned toward Austin.

"Nope."

"You were in the kitchen too?" Sean asked, his voice arching with piqued interest.

"He popped out for a quick smoke. No biggie," Trinity answered on Austin's behalf.

"Out through the door off the kitchen?" Sara asked.

"Yep."

A security guard should have been on the exit, but she asked, "It locks behind you, right?" She grasped for the killer to be some unknown party. It was easier to think about than accepting someone on their guest list was a killer.

Austin shrugged. "Think so. Not sure. I know it closed behind me."

Sara would check that for herself. "And you're sure of that?"

Austin's eyes widened some, and his mouth twitched. "I, uh, now I'm not sure about that. But there was a guy out there, standing guard."

"You probably did, babe," Trinity said and waved a hand of dismissal. "You know what it's like when you're asked something like this… You hem and haw, second-guess yourself. Did I? Didn't I? It's a sure ticket to nutty town."

Either Trinity didn't grasp the potential weight of this, or she was making light of it hoping Sara and Sean would do the same. But if the latter, why?

"You said your aunt wasn't feeling well. Was it her stomach?" Sara asked.

"Cramps." Trinity pulled a face of disgust. "Talk about a case of TMI. Wait. Does it have to do with how she died?"

Sara shook her head. "Doesn't appear so." That's where she'd leave the topic unless the girl asked for specifics. "The police will ask this too, but can you think of anyone who might have wanted to hurt your aunt?" It was an uncomfortable question to ask but was necessary. Sara's mind wasn't far from what she'd overheard Darlene say at the rehearsal dinner. She'd obviously been upset with someone. Her words had been, 'Leave me alone! I have told you it's not happening.' Who had she been saying them to? Did that person turn into her killer today?

Trinity shook her head. "I don't think so."

"There is that company that wanted to buy your aunt's bakery," Austin chimed in. He snapped his fingers. "What was their name again?"

"The Bakery Box."

"Tell us more about them," Sean requested, beating Sara to it. And, surely, he'd heard of them. She certainly had. They had franchises all over the United States.

"I think what he meant was," Sara stepped in, "what were the dealings like with them?"

Sean dipped his head at her, as if to confirm she'd read the intent behind his words.

Trinity faced her boyfriend. "You really think that's relevant, that they killed my aunt? Why?"

"Hmm." Austin's guttural reaction had Sara and Sean looking at him.

"Please, don't keep what you're thinking to yourself," Sean told him.

"Darlene flat out refused to sell to them."

"She had her reasons," Trinity piped up in her aunt's defense.

"Even though they were willing to pay her *a lot* of money," Austin said.

"Not everything is about money," Trinity spat.

I have told you it's not happening... Were Darlene's words directed at someone from the Bakery Box? Had they found their way into the kitchen last night? Austin's suggestion for a motive seemed a little far-fetched, but she'd seen a lot during her time as a cop. Nothing could be discounted unless the evidence didn't support it. "Why didn't she want to sell?"

"You know Aunt Dar, Sara," Trinity said, and it had Sara shrinking inward. She hadn't been very good at staying in touch with everyone in Cotton Spring Falls since she'd moved to Albany. In two years, a lot could change. She hadn't even met Trinity until today.

"In regard to...?" Sara asked, seeking clarity.

"She likes Cotton Spring Falls just as it is. The Bakery Box coming to town would have changed that. More big stores would come sniffing around. She said she'd never sell because they'd take what she worked her entire life for and turn it into some joke franchise. Everything unique about Locally Baked would be gone."

Sara nodded, appreciating that Darlene had put her heart and soul into her business. She'd never had kids; Locally Baked would be her legacy. It made Sara wonder about its fate now. But also in line with the points Trinity had raised, Sara recalled Darlene Day was a staunch supporter of keeping the town as it was. She never seemed interested in advancement or in the town's population growing. One year, when a new subdivision threatened to add a couple thousand people, she'd called council meetings and successfully stopped the project before it gained traction. She had argued and debated how such an increase would tax the municipality's amenities—water, sewer, garbage collection and disposal, among other services. Tack onto that, an influx of people would open the way to increased crime. A point on which Sara's mother would strongly agree.

"This company didn't take well to your aunt's rejection?" Sean asked.

Trinity shook her head. "They sent a lawyer in last week to threaten her. Told her if she refused to sell, they'd come in with a new store and would run her out of business. Tried to tell her she'd have nothing."

Such an unscrupulous way of doing business. It never ceased to amaze her how low people could sink. In this case, she could see through the veneer of the lawyer's threat. If they thought they'd succeed, why continue to hassle Darlene to sell to them? Obviously, they viewed her as stiff enough competition that they wanted her out of the way. Had they gone as far as murder to attain that goal?

Chapter Eight

Sara and Sean spoke with Trinity and Austin a while longer and found out the Bakery Box had first shown interest in Darlene's shop two months ago, but their lawyer had imposed a deadline this past week. The threat being she had to confirm she would sell her shop to them by Monday at the latest or risk being pushed out of business. Had the conglomerate tired of waiting and taken matters into their own hands? With Darlene Day dead, their competition would be eliminated for good.

"Did you find it odd that she never asked what happened to her aunt?" Sean asked Sara once they were alone.

"It could have just been shock and her not thinking straight."

"Possibly. She also might know very well how she died." He lowered his head and raised his eyebrows, his implication clear.

"You're suggesting the girl killed her own aunt?"

"Why not? It's not unheard of. Some people kill their own parents."

"I know, Sean, but… Well, why would she? Darlene took Trinity in when her parents died and she had nowhere else to turn."

"But wasn't this around the time you moved to Albany? It's not like you really know the girl. You just met her today."

He made a valid point, of course, but she just hated to consider Trinity a suspect—at least this early on. "I'd like more information before I make a leap to suspecting her, Sean. It hurts just thinking that she may have turned around and stabbed her aunt in the back after all Darlene did for her." Sara snapped her mouth shut as she realized how callous her words had been.

"You want more to support her as a suspect? She just admitted to being with Darlene within minutes of her death. I agree about motive being unclear, but we might just need time to uncover it."

"And *if* we do uncover it, I'll be happy to revisit this conversation. Trinity could have also heard how Darlene died through the rumor mill. But there is something you should know." Sara shared what she'd overheard the night before. "Darlene couldn't have been talking with Trinity. She told me she was out with her boyfriend."

"That doesn't mean she didn't pop by."

That took him two seconds to knock down... "Sure, but it could have easily been someone from the Bakery Box there harassing her, deadline aside."

"I'll concede to that. There's more digging to do, but you can't argue that Trinity was one of the last to see Darlene Day alive."

"If that's all we're hinging suspicion on, so was I."

Sean angled his head and regarded her as if she were being ridiculous.

"I don't want to make any assumptions. However, with that said, I'm thinking that the secondary kitchen was likely the murder scene. Want to go look? Ryan and his partner are probably still busy upstairs. Crime scene investigators might not have arrived yet." Sara didn't wait for Sean to reply before she started moving.

She entered the smaller kitchen Darlene would have used, Sean behind her.

The space was rectangular, with cabinetry and a counter along the far wall with a sink and a window. And the end of a counter on the left was the side door that led outside. Further to the left was a walk-in pantry where there was also a sub-zero fridge. But in the middle of the room was a long, wheeled stainless-steel counter with some storage cabinets underneath. What stood in front of that pierced Sara's heart.

Their three-tiered wedding cake with its white-and-pink icing sat on a small round table. Sara's gaze landed on the topper—the oblivious bride and groom—and disappointment twisted in her chest. Sean must have sensed her sorrow, likely feeling his own, because he laid a hand on her back. There was no need to say a word. This day certainly couldn't have gone any worse.

Someone cleared their throat. Sara turned to see Officer Gus Simms with the CSFPD.

He hooked his thumbs on the waistband of his uniform pants. "Sara," he said and danced his gaze to Sean. "I'm going to have to ask that you both leave the kitchen. It's being treated as the murder scene."

"That's been confirmed?" Sean asked.

"The evidence indicates that." Gus pointed toward the cake. "Behind it, on the floor."

Sara peeked around the table and found the evidence. A small pool of blood.

The officer cleared his throat again. "As I said, though, Sara, I ask kindly that you both leave the kitchen."

She looked at the door that led outside and moved toward it.

"Sara, please." The officer stepped in front of her.

No light seeped in around the door, and there was no draft. It must be sealed, but was it locked? She was about to turn the handle when Gus spoke.

"Sara. Please." He sounded exasperated.

"Sara." Ryan Doyle echoed her name.

She turned to find him and Louise Farmer. She was scowling. Ryan's eyes were dark beady marbles.

"What are you doing in here?" Ryan didn't seem to acknowledge Sean's presence at all.

She nudged out her chin. "Just checking on things."

He shoved his notepad that he'd had in hand into a back pocket. "There aren't any *things* you need to check on. There is a murder investigation underway, and you're standing where Darlene Day was attacked and contaminating the scene."

"Pretend we were never here." Sean held out a hand for Sara to take.

"Kind of hard to do that," Ryan said stiffly.

"Listen, we didn't touch anything. Just let it go," Sara petitioned.

"Not sure that's wise. What were you doing near that door?" Ryan asked.

"I was wanting to get some fresh air," she said. *Liar, liar, pants on fire.*

"Sara, if I were you, I'd start being more forthcoming. You still have questions to answer as one of the last people to see Ms. Day alive." Ryan wasn't even trying to hide his insinuation.

"If you think I had anything to do with Darlene's death, you're a stupid, stupid man."

"Sticks and stones, love."

Her insides heated with anger, and she squeezed Sean's hand. She nudged out her chin. "I told you all I know. I can't even guess who might have had reason to do this to her, as I've been out of town for a couple of years. You have been around, though. Do you know of anyone with something against her?" Sara turned the tables back on the detective, and he jerked his head slightly, as if he'd been slapped by her remark. She should have given more thought to her words before speaking. There were times when Ryan battled with an inward desire to leave town and a feeling of obligation to stick around for his aging parents, who'd had him later in their lives. "You've chosen to stay in your hometown, Ryan. Many people do," she added, backpedaling.

"Yes, well, it doesn't change the fact Darlene was with you when she took her last breath," he pushed back.

"I can't answer why she was."

"Why are you looking at Sara anyhow? You have obviously pegged this room as where the stabbing took place," Sean interjected. "As you're fond of pointing out, Sara was upstairs. That being when Darlene was stabbed. Three people can verify that she had the knife in her back when she walked into the bridal suite."

Ryan bit his bottom lip and glanced at Louise, then he said, "Yes, well… Family and friends… And the fact remains that Darlene Day didn't take her last breath until she was with you."

"Ryan, you're being ridiculous here," Sara pleaded. *Must I point to the blood on the floor?*

He held up a hand. "Just looking at this objectively. You can go, but don't go far. And I certainly don't want you interfering with my investigation. Am I understood?"

"Yes," she hissed. How had her assessment of Ryan's character been so off the mark? He'd never talked to her like this when she worked with him at the CSFPD. Was it down to jealousy in that she'd chosen Sean? She never would have pegged Ryan as petty. Could there be something else at play?

"Let me get the door for you." Louise was headed that way when the door from the ballroom swung open, and Jimmy came in with Magnum.

The beagle was a relief to see, and Sara bent to her haunches to pet him. His big floppy, soft-as-velvet ears were the best. A sure remedy for any ailment. "Hey, fella."

"For the love of…" Ryan flailed an arm and directed his anger at Gus. "Is it too much to ask that you watch this room from the other side of the door?"

"On it." Gus's cheeks flushed, and he ducked into the ballroom.

"As for you two, or should I say, three—"

"Four," Sara corrected. "Magnum counts."

"Hey, that's a cute name." This from Louise Farmer. The smile lighting her face earned a glare from Ryan.

"Yes, apt, considering he belongs to two former detectives," Sean said.

"Turned sleuth, apparently," Ryan mumbled and pinched the bridge of his nose. He threw a pointed finger toward the door. "Please get out."

Sara resumed her full height and patted her leg for Magnum to follow, but he stood still, his nose raised in the air. He must have caught the whiff of something he found interesting. The cake? Some other food? She tugged gently on his leash to encourage him to move. "Let's go, Magnum."

But he had no interest in obeying. Magnum's nose was taking him away from the door and toward the mobile counter. His sniffing was so hard, he was snorting. He stopped in front of the island, lowering his front end to the floor, while his rear remained high in the air. He swiped his left paw under the counter.

Sara bent down to see what the fuss was about and spotted a small gray feather. One belonging to a dove? Such a strange place to find one of those.

"Sara," Ryan prompted, standing right behind her now.

"Yes, we're leaving." She touched Magnum's head and tapped her thighs for him to get moving. This time he decided he'd go along with her. She took a detour to the rear of the walk-in pantry on the way, having eyed another door there.

"Oh, for goodness' sake," Ryan said.

She ignored him and pushed on the door. It opened into a corridor. She motioned for Sean and Jimmy to join her and Magnum. "Hey, we're leaving—just out this way. Ta-ta." She finger-waved, sounding confident, as if she had a clue where this would lead them, but she had none.

It's an adventure, Harry, she thought, like that line from *Mamma Mia!*

Chapter Nine

Thankfully, Ryan and Louise hadn't been interested in following them. Sara led the way down a narrow corridor lit by mounted sconces allocated every six feet. "I wonder where this goes," she said, speaking her curiosity out loud.

"Guess we'll find out," Jimmy put in. "You should probably stop pushing that detective's buttons, though. Jail, remember? It's a real possible outcome for interfering with a police investigation."

Sara shook her head. "Ryan's hot air. He won't lock us up."

"He might not lock *you* up," Sean said. "By the way, what was Magnum fussing about? Anything important?"

She wasn't too confident Ryan would extend her any leniency. "It was a dove's feather."

"Strange spot. It certainly didn't get there on its own," Jimmy pointed out.

"Thought the same, but that doesn't mean it came from the killer."

"I noticed you left it there," Sean said.

"Well, Ryan wants to run the case, let him do all the work. In the meantime, we could be one step ahead of him."

Magnum was leading the way, nose to the ground. It must have been overwhelming at times having such a powerful sense of smell.

She looked at the carpet, a rich burgundy with a cream pattern that resembled chain links. An irregularity had her stopping to take a closer look. "Make that two… *two* steps ahead of Ryan. I'm quite sure this is blood." She pointed at some dark spots.

The three of them examined the carpet and found more. Blood droplets.

"It seems Darlene was stabbed in the kitchen and walked along here," Sean said. "It appears we're heading in the direction of the suites. If so, we're likely to come to a stairwell soon."

They resumed walking and came to that anticipated flight of stairs. They climbed them and came to a small landing with a door. Sean opened it and was the first to step through. Jimmy followed, then Sara with Magnum.

They were in the upstairs hallway from which the bridal suite branched off.

Sean shut the door to the passageway, and it blended in with the wall—its wainscoting a perfect match. "It disappears and makes the hall look like a dead end."

"Now we know how Darlene got upstairs without others seeing her. Because, surely, she would have caused mass panic if she was spotted with a knife in her back." Sara was still battling with why Darlene hadn't screamed for help instead of coming to the bridal suite. There had to be something significant to what she'd said. *Icing.* Sara still had no idea how to unravel that riddle.

"I don't like any of this, Sara." Jimmy's face was somber. "That eager Detective Doyle has a point. Why did Ms. Day go straight to you? Why not kick up a fuss and call out for help?"

Sara shook her head and put a hand on her stomach. If Darlene thought Sara could help her, she'd failed her miserably.

"No sense prattling off rhetorical questions. It won't get us anywhere. Let's talk about what we know." Sean, always the voice of logic.

The three of them formed a huddle. Magnum was testing the limits of his leash and roaming the hallway, sniffing at the baseboards.

"I'll start," Sean said. "Darlene was last seen by her niece in the kitchen at three forty-five."

"And Darlene knocked on the bridal suite at three fifty-five," Sara said.

"The killer had a ten-minute window?" Jimmy whistled.

"It's definitely tight." Sean shared what they'd learned from Trinity Fields.

"Are we're sure the niece didn't do this?" Jimmy asked.

Sara stiffened. "It's not impossible to think someone else got to Darlene." She wasn't in the mood to debate Trinity's innocence or guilt right now.

"The killer couldn't have been far behind the niece, then. In ten minutes, Day was stabbed and walked the corridor up to the second floor like we just did," Jimmy countered.

"Again, not impossible," Sara said. "If we never stopped along the way, it would have taken us a minute or less."

"Jimmy's right, and so are you," Sean said. "Tight window. But given the time that Darlene was fixing the icing, the ballroom would have been empty."

"No one to hear her scream. She could have cried for help." Thinking that was disheartening.

"In the vein of objectivity," Sean began, "*if* Trinity or her boyfriend killed Darlene Day, they'd have had more time."

Sara shook her head. "I'm not going there."

"How well do you know the boyfriend?" Jimmy asked her.

Sean looked at her, and she read the unspoken message in his eyes. It was one of empathy, but it bit all the same. She didn't know either of them. "Motive is still unknown," she said.

"It is still early," Sean conceded, then turned to Jimmy. "A background on the guy might help."

He waved a hand. "Oh no. I'm not getting wrapped up in this."

"Too late for that," Sean pointed out. "I'm quite sure Detectives Doyle and Farmer have you pegged as helping us. You didn't exactly put up a protest in the kitchen a moment ago."

"Let me clarify. It's one thing to poke around here. It's another to slip out and run a background."

"How great if you would." Sara smiled at him, knowing the expression typically worked on him.

"No way, miss. You're not manipulating me this time." He shook his head, but his vigor died quickly, and he added, "Fine. I'll think about it."

"Wonderful. His name is Austin Palmer, presumably from Cotton Spring Falls."

"Hmph."

"Thanks, Jimmy." She beamed, happy to be getting her way.

"Don't thank me yet."

She'd let the matter rest for now. But justice was at stake. "Just going to put out a hypothetical. The killer and Darlene could have known each other. That's possibly why Darlene permitted them access to the kitchen—assuming she did. But was it a long-standing rivalry that became heated? Next thing, well, Darlene gets a knife to the back."

"Heat of the moment would fit the small window of opportunity," Sean said.

"Do we know what kind of knife was used?" Jimmy asked, and Sara shook her head. "Either way, it would seem the weapon was opportunistic. She was stabbed in a kitchen."

"Adds more support to heat of the moment." Sara figured that was most likely, given what they knew.

"There must be someone who heard the woman cry out," Jimmy said, circling back. "Or saw this person who killed her."

"Even if someone heard her cry out, Darlene would have had to duck into the corridor pretty much right away," Sean said. "But as I said, the ballroom would have been empty with people readying for the ceremony. It's likely there are no eyewitnesses."

Readying for the ceremony… That was another type of stab, but it stole her breath all the same. She talked out a scenario. "The person behind the attack must have been fueled with rage to do such a thing. At the same time, their actions were measured. They only stabbed Darlene once. Was it due to time constraints, someone coming toward the kitchen and fear of being caught?"

"Or an impulse kill by an inexperienced killer," Sean inserted.

She nodded, a sick feeling washing over her. "The killer might not even be here anymore. They could have slipped through the side door off the kitchen without a soul seeing them."

They all fell silent for a few beats.

"Huh. Well, if I were them, that would sound like a smart idea," Sean said.

Her heart was racing. "We'll need to speak with the security guy posted there, see if he saw anyone."

Jimmy shook his head and put his hands on his hips. "Do you guys even hear yourselves? *Let it go.* Leave the investigation with that Ryan kid and his lady partner to take care of."

Sara appreciated Jimmy's concern and the wisdom in his caution, but she felt a personal obligation toward apprehending Darlene's killer.

Jimmy waved a hand. "Never mind this old man. I can see it written all over your face. You're not letting this go."

"Thank you for understanding," she said.

"Oh, I never said I understood."

The door to the bridal suite opened, and Albert Needham and a man Sara assumed was his assistant emerged into the hall with Darlene Day's body on a wheeled gurney.

Jimmy groaned at the sight of Needham, and it was reciprocated by the ME. Sara smirked at their complicated relationship. Though *relationship* was pushing it. They merely tolerated each other for professional reasons.

Sean stepped closer to them. "Do you know the type of knife that was used?"

Needham pinched his lips tightly together and let his gaze drift briefly to Jimmy. Back to Sean, he said, "Are you back on the force, Mr. McKinley? I was under the impression Doyle and Farmer from the Cotton Spring Falls PD were handling the case. I'm sure you can appreciate this is an open investigation, and I'm not permitted to disclose such sensitive information to a civilian. But appreciate it or not, it really doesn't matter. Cheerio." He nudged his head toward his assistant to encourage him to get moving, but Magnum was preventing Needham from stepping forward.

The beagle was sniffing around the ME's ankles.

Needham let out a long-suffering puff of breath. "Someone, please, get this dog out of my way."

"Here, boy," Sara called for the hound, but he wasn't the most obedient dog on the planet. She hadn't decided whether it was down to stubbornness or being too smart for his own good.

Magnum reared back and then pushed his front legs against the gurney. It banged into the wall, and a plastic evidence bag fell onto the floor.

The assistant rushed to pick it up, but Sara caught a glimpse before it was secreted away. She fought to fend off a huge grin. Somehow, she kept it suppressed until the two men started down the stairs.

"Was it just me who caught a peek?" she asked Sean and Jimmy. "Or did you see it too?"

"Oh, I saw it."

"Me too." Sean bent down and rubbed Magnum's head. "Good boy."

Chapter Ten

Darlene Day's murder was sounding like a scenario that could have been concocted in the board game Clue. *The baker, in the kitchen, stabbed with a cake serving knife, by…* And that's where Sara lost the thread.

Jimmy was smiling and shaking his head. "You two really do have golden horseshoes up your—"

Sean clamped a hand on Jimmy's shoulder. "Don't say it, Jimmy."

"A serving knife," he spat.

"Not that you were going to say that." Sara laughed. They could bask in this small victory now that Needham was gone. One random act by Magnum had the evidence bag containing the murder weapon falling to the carpet. What were the chances? It just proved how real life could be stranger than fiction. The beagle's shining moments more than made up for his fits of disobedience. At least some luck was turning in their favor.

"But I think it's safe for us to conclude that the murder was likely one of opportunity."

"Even so," Sean started, "I think you were onto something, Sara, to suggest the killer has history with Darlene. People aren't usually sparked to murder on a first encounter."

"Let's talk this out more," Sara said. "There's that conglomerate. The ultimatum. Had they wanted to speed up the deadline?"

"The who?" Jimmy asked, and Sara explained about the Bakery Box wanting to buy Darlene's shop and the threat to go into competition if Darlene didn't comply and sell her store to them. "You think they're motivated enough to resort to murder?"

"They probably viewed her as stiff competition," Sara said.

"Now, she's really *stiff*." Jimmy's morgue humor landed with a thud. He straightened his bow tie and cleared his throat. "Probably too soon."

Sean held up two fingers close to touching. "I think we need to dissect this. Consider means, motive, and opportunity individually and whittle down suspects from there. Then, it's quite possible it's someone you don't know, Sara. You haven't been around Cotton Spring Falls a lot since you moved to Albany."

"I know." A regret she wished to remedy. "It might be easiest to consider people with possible motive."

"Always start close and branch out," Jimmy put in. "You have the niece, her boyfriend... Did Darlene have a husband or boyfriend?"

"Her husband passed ten years ago now easily, and I've heard Darlene say many times that she was too old to train a new one." Sara smiled at the recollection and winked at Sean. "As to whether she had any romantic entanglements or more casual relationships, that I don't know."

Jimmy hitched his shoulders. "Easy enough to find out. We can just ask the niece if her aunt was seeing anyone. Who else, do you think?"

Sara searched her memory and landed on something. "Last fall, Darlene ran for town council against a man by the name of Henry Travis. He's lived in Cotton Spring Falls all his life too. But he had a very different viewpoint than Darlene."

"He was for advancement?" Sean asked.

Sara nodded and explained to Jimmy. "Darlene liked Cotton Spring Falls the way it is, and it's why she didn't want some franchise moving in. To her, it would mark the beginning of the end of the town she loved."

"And did she win the vote?" Jimmy asked.

"Darlene? You bet. She was a powerhouse." Sara paused, caught up in memories of the woman.

"The vote was last fall, though," Jimmy began. "Even if it irked him to lose, why kill Darlene now?"

"You said he grew up in town, Sara," Sean said. "He might have tired of people resisting his forward thinking and decided to get rid of the woman leading them."

"Oh, Henry has his own band of supporters," she said.

"Then any of them could have been unhappy that Darlene was slowing the progress of Cotton Spring Falls," Sean said. "And the Bakery Box just started buzzing around a couple of months ago."

"Huh." Jimmy's face shadowed. "Was it widespread knowledge that they approached her?"

"Unsure, but I can't imagine Darlene keeping quiet about it." Sara had always known Darlene to speak her mind fully and unabashedly.

"That may have resurrected things for Henry Travis and his contingents," Jimmy said.

Sean turned to Sara. "How many people are we talking?"

"Probably a few thousand."

"How many on our guest list?"

Sara couldn't meet Sean's eyes. She had that number at the top of her head, and if one of them had killed Darlene, she'd never forgive herself. "Three. Molly Luna. Sean, you met her. She owns Molly's Fine Finds, the vintage store." They'd been introduced when she and Sean needed costumes to go undercover in the case of the murdered bowler.

"Yes, I remember her."

"This Molly owns a business and is also in favor of advancement? She might not have been too happy that Darlene, her fellow businesswoman, was holding back progress." Jimmy flailed his arm.

"Then there's her best friend, Gertie Smith." Sara was having a hard time sizing up Molly or Gertie as killers.

"And…?" Sean peered into her eyes.

"Hugh Thornton."

"Our master of ceremonies? Also your former sergeant?"

"Yes. But I can't see any of them hurting a fly."

"Ryan might be going hard on us because Thornton told him to," Sean said. "He might not want Darlene's murder solved—because he killed her."

Sean's theory was a punch to her gut. "I need to…" She paced. "Sit down."

Sean held on to her arm and buoyed her. Jimmy remained quiet for a few beats, which she appreciated.

"You won't want to hear this, Sara, but we need to speak with all of them," Sean said.

"Due diligence." It didn't mean she wouldn't hate scrutinizing those nearest and dearest to her, eyeing them up as cold-blooded murderers.

"Oh, Sara, there you are." Her mother reached the landing and beelined toward her. "People are getting restless and hungry now. What are we going to do?"

Sara put a hand on her mother's forearm. "You need to let the police do their work."

Jeannie's shoulders relaxed. "Well, I am happy to hear you say that. Does that mean you're leaving this alone, letting the police handle the investigation?" She traced her eyes over the three of them.

Jimmy shied away from her gaze, Sean pressed his lips, and Sara flashed an expression that was somewhere between a smile and a wince.

"Oh, Sara." Jeannie dropped her arms heavily at her side as if she had lost all power to hold them up any longer.

"Excuse me." A man bellowed from the main level, and his voice traveled up the stairs. "Could I have everyone's attention? Please make your way to the ballroom."

"That has to be an officer," Sara said. The ballroom made more sense than the dining hall from an investigative standpoint. There was less seating, and the more uncomfortable people were, the more eager they were to talk so they could get going.

Sean cupped her elbow. "You go with your mother and Jimmy. I'm going to see if I can take Magnum, sneak outside, and have a look around."

"Dear heavens," Jeannie groaned.

"She's right," Jimmy interjected. "If you're caught…"

"Orange jumper." Jeannie must have filled out the picture just in case Sean missed Jimmy's implication.

"Innocent enough explanation." Sean lifted Magnum's leash, which Sara had passed over to him. "Magnum's my cover story. Dogs need to go out to do their business."

"Brilliant." Sara pecked a kiss on Sean's cheek, and he spun toward her and scooped his arm around her waist.

"I want a proper kiss," he said, and then he gave her one.

When he pulled away, she was flooded with warmth and sorrow. If only things had gone as planned. But someone had a far worse day than she was having. Couldn't that always be said, though? Was that reason enough to put off happiness or play up troubles—to make others comfortable? A deep thought worthy of picking up another time.

"Everyone in the ballroom," the same man repeated, his baritone again flooding the second floor.

"What are you going to do?" Sara asked Sean.

"I'll take the passageway and go out through the side door off the kitchen," he said.

"But there's an officer posted there. Crime scene investigators might be buzzing around by this point too." Jimmy's brow was creased into rows of wrinkles, his fifty-plus years clear in the folds of skin.

"I will take the chance." Sean headed toward the door for the hidden passageway.

"But do you need to?" Sara asked. "You have Magnum."

"I'm only going to use the cover story if necessary." With that, Sean kissed Sara's lips, then tucked inside the hidden corridor with Magnum. The door had just shut as a uniformed officer reached them.

"Folks, I need you in the ballroom," he said.

Sara led the way down with her mother, Jimmy following. She'd have gladly exchanged places with Sean, but she'd find ways to keep herself busy.

Chapter Eleven

Sean must have been a touch insane—or a whole lot in love—to keep going with this investigation. Jail time was an all-too-real possibility for him. It was clear Detective Doyle had it out for him. Sean mentally coached himself to calm down. *No one is going to jail…* He'd cling to that as he justified his actions. As soon as Darlene Day's killer was found, he could get on with marrying the woman of his dreams. That kiss they'd just shared had been all the added fuel he needed to keep going.

He and Magnum made it through the passageway at a decent clip. There were blood drops, supposedly belonging to Darlene, but he wasn't too concerned about contaminating evidence against the killer here. There was nothing to indicate they had given chase after the woman. Sara's theory about the killer sneaking out held a lot of potential, though wasn't absolute. The one flaw in that supposition was they suspected the person who killed Darlene had known her—and him and Sara. Would they risk their absence being noted?

Fearful self-talk amped up when he reached the door that entered the kitchen. He had no idea what might be waiting for him.

He pressed his ear against the wood. Heard nothing. Good sign. CSIs must have either finished and left or hadn't arrived yet, and the uniformed officer had moved to the ballroom outside the kitchen door.

Time to move...

He hesitated a few seconds. Still surrounded by silence, he looked down at Magnum. "All right, buddy. It's go time."

Sean twisted the door handle, about to push, when he heard voices. If he guessed right, it was Doyle and his partner.

The soles of their shoes slapped against the kitchen floor and were coming right for him.

Sean turned and started running down the passageway, retracing his earlier steps through the corridor to upstairs. As he moved, he had empathy for how rabbits or groundhogs must feel when they were cornered in their burrows.

What if officers were waiting at the other end? Though none had been when he'd left. That left the main staircase, and there was likely a uniform posted at the base. He might test that cover story after all.

He hurried his pace a bit more, the entire time praying no officers were upstairs. While he had a valid excuse to go outside, he would be short of an explanation to justify his presence in the corridor and upper hallway.

His ear against the other door, he listened closely. The hallway was quiet, but he heard Doyle and Farmer talking behind him. They were in the corridor, leaving Sean no choice but to continue forward.

He stepped out into the hallway and let out a deep breath. No one was there.

Softly shutting the passageway door behind him, he considered his next move. Go down and potentially use his cover story, or face off with Doyle. The choice seemed easy to make, but Sean remained frozen.

The detectives' voices were drawing close. Doyle and his partner would exit the corridor at any moment. Sean had even run out of time to explain himself to an officer on the main level—if there was one at the base of the stairs. Doyle and Farmer would be close enough to overhear him now.

Think, McKinley, think!

The passageway door started to swing open.

Time is up!

Sean tucked inside the bridal suite with Magnum, gently closing the door behind him. *Now what?*

He tried to calm himself down. The detectives already spent time in the suite. Surely, they'd just keep walking or turn back around—

The handle on the suite's door rattled as it turned.

Shoot!

Scanning the room, Sean had one option—the closet. He had less than a second to register that it held Sara's wedding dress before he and Magnum squeezed inside. They barely fit.

Doyle and Farmer moved around the room.

Please don't open the closet, please don't open the closet… He'd chant it like a mantra if it would help.

"The vic must have used the passageway," Farmer said.

"Further confirmation that the kitchen is the murder scene."

Sean rolled his eyes. As if more than a pool of blood on the tile floor was needed…

"We have that woman's testimony too," Farmer started. The rustling of pages being turned in a notepad, then, "Nora Ward."

"Yes. She overheard the vic arguing in the kitchen. Just not with who. Not entirely helpful," Doyle said, his voice carrying the tinge of a whine.

"It tells us someone wasn't happy with the vic."

"Really, Louise? Bravo. The knife in the back gave that away. We need more."

"Ward said she checked on the situation, but no one was in the kitchen," Farmer replied, not missing a beat despite her ignorant partner.

"Yep, vanished into thin air!"

"The vic retreated into the passageway."

"And the killer?" Doyle muttered.

"Ward heard someone walking away, dragging their one leg behind, their shoe scuffing against the floor."

"But saw no one."

Coming into this room was paying off. Sean had just picked up a lead. Now to find someone with motive who had an uneven gait. It might also be advantageous to speak with this Nora Ward for themselves.

Sean shuffled slightly and cringed when the tip of his shoe banged against the door of the closet. He held his breath and waited. But it didn't seem that either detective had heard him. Thank heaven for small mercies.

"We should get downstairs," Doyle said. "Everyone should be gathered in the ballroom by now."

"I'm with you. But don't you think you're going a bit hard on Sara and Sean? This was their wedding day."

There was a stretch of silence.

"I need to remain objective, Louise. You know that."

"Yeah, and the sarge isn't making our lives easy right now either."

Sean wanted to shout, *in what way*, but he wouldn't dare.

Doyle and Farmer left and closed the suite door behind them. Sean waited a few seconds before he emerged from his hidey-hole with Magnum. He rubbed the beagle's ears while the hound soaked up the affection. "Good fella."

Sean peeked his head into the hall, and no one was within sight. Steps thumped on the staircase.

Sean stepped out of the bridal suite, and Magnum paced around Sean's legs. The cover story just became the truth. "A few more minutes, buddy."

The detectives left the passageway door open, and Sean and Magnum walked through.

No sounds were traveling up the corridor.

Score!

Sean picked up speed. He stood and listened at the kitchen door like before. Not a peep.

He turned the handle, stuck his head in. No one in sight.

They stepped into the kitchen, and Sean led Magnum to the side door. He wondered if the killer had done the same. It would be helpful to know in which direction that person with the bum leg had gone.

The door hit resistance, and there was an "Ouch" followed by a grunt.

Sean eased up and pushed again with caution. It wasn't a police officer he'd hit but a security guard's back.

The man flinched at the sight of Sean and put some space between them.

Sean held up his hands. "Sorry. I didn't mean to scare you there—or hit you with the door."

"No problem. My apologies, Mr. McKinley." The man spoke robotically, and his eyes stared through Sean.

Sean wasn't surprised he knew his name, because the security team would have been briefed and given his and Sara's photographs. He had no reason to apologize, though. Without police present, he could use this opportunity to ask some questions. "Slow night at this post?"

"Yep."

Sean waited a few beats, curious if the man would elaborate. When he didn't, Sean spoke again. "You've been here all afternoon and evening thus far?"

The man put a hand on his hip above his holster. "I have."

Not a person of many words, and he was still eyeing Sean for whatever reason. "Did anyone come out from inside… well, besides me?"

"Yes. A young man for a cigarette earlier."

Okay, that is good… "Anyone else not long after that?"

"Nope. Just me. Well, except there was Mr. Voigt a couple hours ago, after the…"

Sean nodded, not about to make the man say *murder.* Most people weren't comfortable with the topic. "All right, well, keep up the good job." He moved to step around the guard, but he shuffled in front of Sean at the same time. "Sorry about that," Sean said.

"Don't be—"

"Mr. McKinley? What are you doing out here?" It was a uniformed officer, someone else armed with his photograph obviously, as Sean hadn't met him before. He was with a buddy too.

The security guard stepped aside and took up his post—though to the opposite side of the door. He clasped his hands in front of his chest, shoulders back and squared. An imposing character and perfect for security detail.

"Just out here for this little guy," Sean told the officers, gesturing toward Magnum.

Both officers barely acknowledged the hound.

"I shouldn't be much longer." But as he was speaking, Magnum betrayed him. He whizzed against the building.

"Seems like business may just be concluding." One officer made the crack and hit his buddy in the arm. He didn't seem amused.

"Very sorry for your ruined day," that officer said.

"Thank you."

"I'll need to ask that you go back inside. Detective Doyle wants everyone in the ballroom," the comedic officer said.

"Righty-ho, well, off I go." He headed toward the door he'd exited with Magnum in tow. *Righty-ho?* He was falling into another persona; he blamed the sleuthing.

The guard held the door for Sean and Magnum to walk through. Sean hadn't known what he'd uncover by going outside, but he got more than he had expected. Even if the answer wasn't savory. Only Austin had used the side door. That meant either he was the killer or someone else had stabbed Darlene Day and hung around and was currently inside the building. But why risk staying when an escape route was so conveniently located?

Just as the question fired, an epiphany hit. It was quite possible that whoever killed Darlene would be greatly missed if they weren't here. The scant thought occurred to him before, but it still had a knot bunching in his chest.

That would put Darlene's niece and her boyfriend directly in the frame. Trinity would be sought for notification. Sara wasn't going to like the way he was leaning.

Chapter Twelve

There could be a murderer in this very ballroom. The thought was as crushing as it was overwhelming. A total of four hundred and twenty-five RSVPs. Seeing the throng in one space, she'd say they all turned up. But just how trustworthy was their security? There was the possibility of loopholes. Had someone snuck in? A stranger was easier to accept than thinking one of their nearest and dearest had murdered Darlene.

Sara was standing with her parents and bridesmaids, scanning the crowd, looking for unfamiliar faces, though she realized rather quickly how that wouldn't do her much good. While she knew the people she'd invited, she wouldn't know all their dates by sight. Had one of them been Darlene's killer? Again, it was easier to consider the person wasn't someone close to her and Sean.

She looked out for anyone who was paying her particular attention—a tough feat, as she was the bride whose wedding day was ruined. Every set of eyes was on her. But during her time in Homicide, she'd learned some killers liked the challenge that came with squaring off with law enforcement. Even if it led to their own detriment. Then again, would the killer view her, Sean, or Jimmy as a threat? They weren't tasked with the case. Jimmy was outside his jurisdiction, and she and Sean no longer had badges.

With Sean in her thoughts, she wondered if he'd discovered anything useful to the investigation. Though it felt like too much to hope that he'd stumbled upon a vital clue that would tighten cuffs around the killer's wrists, she wanted to believe he had.

Uniformed officers from the Cotton Spring Falls PD were making their way around the room, talking to everyone and recording their responses in their notebooks.

She couldn't pluck out Molly, Gertie, or her former sergeant, Hugh Thornton. Three present who had potential motive. But was silencing Darlene's advocacy for keeping the town as it was worth killing over?

"I hope they're not going to keep us here all night," a man said to the woman next to him.

When Sara met his eye, he offered an insincere smile and couldn't seem to be bothered to show any apology for his selfish statement or empathy for how Sara must be feeling about the day's direction. He might not know who she was. She didn't recognize him. It was the woman next to him Sara had invited. Tammy Plunket. She was a widow who lived two doors down from her parents' place, but she also used to babysit Sara when she was a child. The man must have been her date.

Sara gave Tammy a pressed-lip smile.

"Such a tragedy. I'm sorry this has happened, Sara," Tammy told her. At least she had the decency to blush at the poor manners of her date.

The man stood straighter and tugged down on his suit jacket once he clued into who Sara was. "I apologize if you heard me just now."

Sara merely dipped her head. He knew very well she'd heard him. To Tammy, she said, "I appreciate that, but I feel for Darlene's niece."

"Yes, that poor girl. Say, looks like she's coming this way." Tammy flicked a pointed finger across the room.

Sure enough, Trinity was weaving through the crowd, heading toward Sara with her boyfriend, Austin, in her wake.

"Sara." One word, but Trinity's voice shook.

"What is it?" Sara gently touched her forearm. Sara's mother groaned beside her, but Sara ignored it. "Let's talk over here." She guided Trinity out of her mother's earshot.

"He's here," Trinity said.

"Who?" Sara darted her gaze about the room as if she could magically spot the person under discussion.

"The man from the Bakery Box."

"The one who issued the deadline?" Sara's skin prickled with goose bumps. He certainly hadn't been on the guest list.

"Yes."

"Where is he?"

"Right there. Balding, glasses." Trinity pointed him out.

Sara followed the direction of Trinity's finger, and her gaze landed on a middle-aged man matching the girl's description. He also had a small paunch. She turned back to Trinity. "What's his name? Do you know?"

"Ah, it's…" Trinity snapped her fingers, pressed her lips, bounced on her heels. "Ralph Patrick."

Never trust a person with two first names… Did the adage hold merit? "Okay, stay here. I'm going to talk to him." Sara made one step in that endeavor, and her mother caught her arm on a backswing. "Please. Let me go, Mom."

"You're not leaving this to the police." Obvious disapproval was served with the allegation.

Sara steadied herself. Her mother's constant nagging on this topic was growing old. Fast. "Mom, it's fine. I'll be fine."

Her mother frowned, concern seeping into her eyes.

Sara knew Jeannie had her best interests at heart, but Sara was wired for investigating. It was in her blood, whether or not she was on the police force. "I'll be fine," she repeated and walked toward Ralph.

A few feet away, Sean and Magnum intercepted.

She put her arms around Sean's neck and nuzzled her mouth close to his ear. "Did you discover anything?"

"Long story there, but I think our killer may have an uneven gait, possibly a bum leg or sore knee," he said toward her earlobe. "I overheard Doyle and Farmer talking."

Sara mentally scrolled the invitation list and couldn't think of anyone who fit that description. It was possible that the killer recently injured themselves or stumbled. It may also be a plus-one brought by a guest. She wasn't familiar with them all. "Anything else?" She was greedy for answers.

They backed out of their embrace but stood close.

"I spoke to the security guard posted at the side door. No one went out there, Sara, except for Austin and Jimmy. The killer is here. Likely in this very room."

Her head spun, but she coached herself to calm down. Before Sean's update, there was the possibility the killer had ducked out the side door.

Magnum pawed at Sara's leg, and she reached down and rubbed his head.

"You looked like you were on your way to do something when we waylaid you," Sean said.

"I was just going to talk to—" She looked past Sean, seeking out Ralph Patrick, but she couldn't see him anymore. He had moved, though he couldn't have gone far.

"Who, Sara?" he prompted.

"Ralph Patrick. He's the rep from the Bakery Box who threatened Darlene and imposed the Monday deadline. He was right there." She nudged her head in the direction of where he had been.

"And now he's gone? Huh, that's convenient, but he couldn't have gone far. Officers are at the doors."

"I suppose. Just so you know, he's middle-aged, slightly paunchy, with a balding head and glasses."

"I'll keep an eye out for him."

"Sean, he wasn't on the guest—"

"Sara Cain? Sean McKinley?" A woman interrupted Sara, and it had her and Sean turning in unison.

Sara didn't need to see the face to place the voice. "Desiree Moore, what are you doing here?" No sense stating the blatantly obvious that the *New York Times* reporter hadn't been invited.

Desiree's eyes dipped to Magnum before she looked up and ogled Sean. "Well, I was here to cover your wedding, but it seems that's been delayed… or postponed?"

Sean grimaced at the unwanted attention. "You will be leaving now." He grabbed her by the arm and started to usher her toward the ballroom doors.

"Wait," Sara called out.

"Sara, she's not welcome."

"I know," she said to Sean and walked right up to Desiree's nose. "How did you get in here?"

Desiree smirked. "Wouldn't you like to know?"

"We're not playing games here, Ms. Moore," Sean said firmly. "There's been a murder, and you're not on the guest list. I'm sure the detectives working the case would love to have a chat with you."

"Oh, please. I didn't kill anyone, but I do hear a lot. Things you might be interested in knowing."

Sara took a few breaths, drawing on her patience, which was typically one of her strengths. Desiree always put it to the test. "Like what?"

Desiree smiled, the cat who ate the canary. "I'll tell you. In exchange for exclusive rights to cover your wedding when it does happen."

Always out for her own agenda. Sara opened her mouth to speak, but Sean beat her to it.

"If it's about the murder, you need to talk to us."

"That's where you are wrong. You and Sara are not police anymore, Mr. McKinley."

"Then I'll take you to some. We'll see what they think of you holding back information on an open investigation." Sean reached for her arm again, but she juked out of his reach.

"Fine." Desiree held up her hands. "I overheard this woman telling Detective Doyle that she heard an argument in the kitchen between the victim and someone else."

"Nora Ward," Sean supplied, and Sara turned to him. She knew Nora quite well.

"That's her." Desiree's eyes narrowed, fear showing that she might have lost her advantage. "But here's the thing… She told the police that she heard a man walking away, scuffing a shoe behind him."

"A man? Are you sure?" Sean asked.

"That's what she told the cops. But I overheard her talking to your mother, Sara. She said she heard who the victim was arguing with moments before… well, you know. From what I've gathered, she'd withheld that from the police."

The back of Sara's neck and arms were tingling. "Did she say who it was?"

A slight smirk, one eyebrow raised. "The victim's niece."

"You're lying," Sara spat.

"I assure you I speak the absolute truth. Cross my heart and hope to die." She mimicked a wince. "Maybe that was a little cold given the circumstances."

"Ya think?" Sean said drily.

"When was this?" Sara's head was spinning processing what she was hearing. Had her trust in Trinity been misplaced, unwarranted? After all, as she'd admitted to Sean, she didn't know her. She just didn't want to accept that someone related to Darlene was capable of murder.

"It was around three thirty, maybe a bit earlier."

Sara glanced at Sean. Based on what Trinity had told them, she and her boyfriend weren't in the kitchen until quarter to four. That was fifteen minutes after Nora supposedly heard aunt and niece arguing. Nora could have gotten the time wrong.

Still, what was Trinity doing in the kitchen? Was it just as Trinity had said, and she was checking in on her aunt? Possibly collecting her for the ceremony? But it wouldn't seem Darlene left with them. Had she told her niece and Austin to go ahead and that she'd follow?

But Nora had lied about a man dragging his leg. What's to say she wasn't lying about Trinity too? Still, why share a different version of events with Jeannie? If Sara didn't know better, she'd suspect Nora, but she was harmless and held no ill will toward Darlene. She was even on her side for keeping Cotton Spring Falls as it was.

Sara spotted Nora in one of the chairs that lined the room. She was pale-faced, and her eyes were zigzagging all over. "Sean, we need to speak with Nora."

"Ooooh. Are you two investigating?" Desiree's eyes widened with excitement. "Look at you, a pair of billionaire sleuths."

Sean stepped in front of Desiree. "And you're going to keep quiet about it."

"I am? Why would I do that?"

"I assume you'd love those exclusive rights to cover our wedding," he volleyed back, then looked over his shoulder and mouthed an apology to Sara. Sometimes it was necessary to make a deal with the devil, as was the media, but he'd just dangled the carrot. Technically, no promises were made.

Desiree mimed zipping her lips.

"You never did tell us how you got in," Sara said.

Desiree pointed at her mouth to imply it was too late for that. Her lips were sealed.

"Very well. We'll figure it out on our own." Sara never did care much for the woman, but that feeling only grew stronger with every interaction.

Chapter Thirteen

Sara and Sean walked over with Magnum to Nora Ward. It occurred to Sara that, according to Desiree, the woman had confided in Jeannie. Had her mother gone to Ryan? For her caution to Sara to watch her actions, did her mother not realize withholding information pertinent to the investigation could get *her* into trouble?

"Desiree Moore must have paid a security guard to let her in," Sean said, keeping pace with Sara.

"I thought Jimmy vetted all of them."

"You know how it goes sometimes."

She nodded. Not everyone can be trusted. Sad but true, and she still longed to believe in people. "Even so." She smiled at Nora when she reached her.

"Oh, Sara." Nora extended her legs as if she were going to stand but tucked them back. It was also telling body language that she was retreating inward, possibly prepared to be defensive. In the least, she was uncomfortable.

"Hello, Nora. Have you met Sean?" Sara gestured toward him.

"Hi, ah, nice to meet you."

Sean reached to shake her hand, and Nora awkwardly complied. But she wasn't one to stand on formal etiquette. The saying that some people are like earthworms for their down-to-earth natures fit Nora perfectly. But it was one of her best qualities. A person always knew where they stood with her.

"Who's this little guy?" Nora scratched Magnum's back, and he wriggled with pleasure.

Sara smiled. "Magnum."

"Well, hello there, Magnum." Nora spoke in baby talk.

"Nora, Sean and I were hoping to speak with you."

"Isn't that what we're doing?" As Nora's eyes locked with Sara's, they dimmed. "This is about Darlene and what I heard?"

"It is."

"Don't have much to tell."

Not how we hear it…

"It might be better to take this conversation"—Sean looked around—"over there." He indicated a quiet corner of the room.

"Sure."

The group of them moved there.

"We heard the police questioned you," Sara began.

"Yes, and what a stressful thing that was."

"You heard something, just moments before Darlene was murdered?" Sean asked.

"I am sorry to admit that. But yes." Nora's body language became rigid, guarded.

"Will you tell us what that was?" Sara wanted to hear it from Nora's own lips.

"An argument."

Sean angled his head. "What gave you that impression? Did you hear something specific? Perhaps what it was about?"

"I wish I heard something useful, but I couldn't make out any words. I only could tell it was an argument from the volume and how things were being said."

"I see." Darlene had been vocal, exuberant, and some might have seen her as overbearing. For Darlene's inflection in her speech to be what triggered Nora to check on her, it must have been quite a heated conversation. According to Desiree's retelling, it had been between Darlene and her niece. Nora hadn't yet mentioned Trinity, but it was best not to rush these things along. "What time was this?"

"Around three thirty, give or take a few minutes. I was standing in the ballroom by myself. You know how I can be sometimes, Sara."

She nodded. "Nora likes her personal space," she added for Sean's benefit.

"And peace and quiet."

"You're sure it was around three thirty? Any way it could have been later?" Sara was interested to see the strength of Nora's conviction.

"Definitely within minutes of three thirty."

If that was the case, Trinity had gone in prior to three forty-five on her own and failed to let her and Sean know about that. Regardless, Darlene was alive until mere minutes to four. "Did you check out the noise? Make sure Darlene was okay?"

"I did."

Sara lit at that. No one had said Nora had *seen* something. "So you entered the kitchen?"

"Uh-huh."

How many layers would she need to work through to reach the extent of what Nora had witnessed? "Was anyone with her?"

"No one."

"No one?" Sara parroted back, a swell of disappointment rising within her at the lie. Why was Nora holding back from them? "Are you sure about that?"

"Yes."

"So Darlene was arguing with herself, is that it?" Sean raised his eyebrows—his skepticism apparent.

Nora's shoulders slumped.

"You had to have seen someone with Darlene," Sara said in a kind manner.

Nora opened her mouth but then pursed her lips. Her eyes briefly darted past Sara, in Sean's direction.

"Ms. Ward, you can talk to us," Sara added, appealing to her old babysitter.

"I trust you, Sara, but why are you and Sean asking me about all this? I feel wretched as it is. Darlene must have been murdered just moments after I saw her." Nora rubbed her brow, and Magnum whimpered and drew their attention. He was peering up at Nora with the expressive eyes of a hound. She petted his head.

"We're sorry to put you through this," Sara said. "We're just trying to figure out who might have done this to her."

"Sara, I didn't think you were police anymore."

"We're not, but this murder happened at our wedding," Sara said. "I'm sure you can appreciate how this would make us very interested in its resolution."

Nora frowned, and Sara heard her words play back in her head.

"That sounded much colder than intended." Sara paused, upset over the fact she hadn't measured her words as diligently as she normally did prior to speaking. "I've known Darlene all my life."

Nora pointed a finger at Sara. "Except for the last two years."

A jab at Sara's move to "the big city" of Albany. "My parents still live here, and I've been around." It might be time for Sara to push this conversation along. "We've heard a rumor… Now it might not be true." She'd leave her mother and Desiree's names out of this.

"You should never pay much heed to rumors, Sara. You should know that."

"Yes, Ms. Ward, but this one comes on good authority." *Does it?* She hated the tingle of doubt that moved in. Desiree Moore was a self-serving individual, a person who loved to stir up drama if it resulted in a good headline.

"Very well. Your mother said something?"

Sara shook her head and remained silent. Doing so was stronger than anything she could have said.

"Who did you see?" Sean eventually prompted.

Nora moved in close to Sara and whispered, "Trinity Fields."

Finally! Why had it been such a struggle to get Nora to divulge that?

"She's Darlene's niece, Sara."

"I am well aware." The timing still needed to be reconciled. "Without a doubt, niece and aunt were arguing?" The pit of Sara's stomach was swirling.

"Without a doubt," Nora parroted. "But they both fell silent when they saw me."

"They didn't want you to hear what they had been discussing," Sara concluded.

"It was obviously personal, so I excused myself."

"Before that, did you see anything else? *Anyone* else?" Sean asked.

"No, but didn't I see enough?"

Based on her pained expression, Nora had convicted Trinity Fields in her mind. "Where were they standing?" Sara wanted to flesh out the scene.

"Near the sink. Why does that matter?"

Sara wouldn't tell Nora, but it might matter. *Might* being quite the contingency. The blood pool, and therefore, presumably the stabbing had taken place next to the cake. That was on a pedestal several feet from the sink—the opposite side of the center counter. It was possible, after Nora excused herself, the argument moved across the room. "Do you know what Darlene and her niece were doing at the sink?" She'd learned it was better to ask too many questions than not enough. Sometimes the most surprising answers held the key to solving the case.

"I think Darlene was washing something up. I heard something clink against the steel sink."

The niece had told them Darlene needed to touch up the icing. It was feasible when Nora had entered the kitchen that had already been done and Darlene was washing up. Sara hadn't taken note of any dishes—clean or otherwise—sitting out.

Nora let out a deep sigh, and Sara studied her closely. She was paler than a few moments ago, and her face was more drawn. If Sara wasn't imagining things, she was also slightly trembling. "Why didn't you tell the police you saw Trinity?" Sara carefully posed the question so as not to come across judgmental.

The woman's eyes met Sara's. "How do you know I didn't?"

"Please just tell me why." Sara hoped the earnest appeal would stir something deep inside the woman to remind her of the young girl she used to care for.

"You never heard this from me."

The hairs rose on the back of Sara's neck, and her ears perked up. Something juicy always followed this caveat. "We'll keep it to ourselves." Sara gestured toward Sean, who nodded, adding his affirmation.

"Trinity and her aunt didn't exactly see eye to eye. Trinity wanted to attend this fancy college in New York. You might have noticed that she's a petite, little thing. She's a rather incredible ballerina, so said Darlene even, and the girl wanted to apply to Juilliard."

"Darlene wasn't on board," Sara surmised.

"Not at all. She wanted to pass Locally Baked on to Trinity. She was her only living relative."

Sara hated what this was telling her. With Darlene dead, her money was likely set to go to Trinity. She'd be free to go to Juilliard or do anything else she wished.

Nora continued. "I don't have to tell you, but Darlene worked hard to build that bakery into what it is today. It's years of her blood, sweat, and tears that got the attention of that big-box bakery." Nora waved a hand of dismissal and disgust at just mentioning them.

The fact Nora knew Darlene had refused to sell only confirmed that it would be common knowledge among the long-time residents of Cotton Spring Falls. That also meant those who opposed Darlene's resistance to growth would have heard about the Bakery Box's offer. Her mind regurgitated Molly Luna, Gertie Smith, and Sergeant Thornton—three in attendance who were pro-advancement. Regardless, they were just as unlikely to kill Darlene as her own niece. Then again, does anyone fully know another person's heart?

Sean glanced briefly at Sara before looking at Nora. "Tell us more about that man with a bum leg. How does he fit in?"

"About that..." Nora bit her bottom lip, and that churning in Sara's gut sped up. "I will confess to you that was a lie. Now, I'm not very proud of myself for that, but residents of Cotton Spring Falls do what they must to protect each other."

Even protect a killer? The thought fired through Sara's mind, and she felt she'd betrayed Trinity Fields. Still, she said, "Darlene Day lived in Cotton Spring Falls all her life. What about protecting her?"

"There is no sense in ruining two lives, and I don't know if that girl killed Darlene. The police don't always take the time to step back and look objectively—even when the lead is one of our own. If I gave her name over to Ryan Doyle, he'd crucify her and be blind to any other possibility."

Sara didn't remember the woman being so skeptical, but she was having a harder time considering Trinity Fields as their prime murder suspect—the victim's own niece, her only blood relative. To play devil's advocate, though, there were still missing pieces. "After you walked in on them, where did you go afterward?" Sara was thinking if she'd simply returned to the ballroom, she might have seen someone else join Darlene in the kitchen—after Trinity and Austin left.

"I ended up going to the main hall. It was almost time for the ceremony. So sorry all this happened, Sara."

At that moment, Sara wasn't sure how much that apology covered or its main intent—the lying and deceit to the police, or her and Sean's ruined wedding. She simply dipped her head and touched the woman's shoulder. "Thank you for talking with us."

"You're welcome."

Sara should have admonished Nora to come clean to Ryan with everything she had just told them, but she didn't see a point in wasting her breath. Nora made it clear how she felt about him. None of this would stop Sara from questioning Trinity Fields again, though. One benefit to Ryan knowing nothing about any of this was what he didn't know couldn't hurt her.

Chapter Fourteen

Sean appreciated why Sara didn't want to take this information to Doyle. Nora had made a point about it potentially blinding Doyle to other possibilities. Also, if they shared what they'd learned with Doyle, he'd accuse them of poking around, and that would land them in trouble. Sean already suspected that their master of ceremonies, Sergeant Thornton, might not be too thrilled either. Based on what he overheard Doyle and his partner say, he took it to mean that he and Sara were being given a tough time because of him. And as Jeannie stressed repeatedly—and even Jimmy mentioned at least twice—interfering in the investigation was a crime, and it could get them fined, or worse, imprisoned. Sean wasn't particularly interested in either outcome.

Trinity was with Austin in a corner of the room, his arm around her waist. She had that deer-in-the-headlights look to her—eyes wide and wet. A glass of water was in her hand, and it shook when she raised it for a sip.

"Did you talk to that man, Sara?" Trinity asked, and Sean assumed she meant the rep from the Bakery Box.

Sara frowned and shook her head. "I haven't caught up with Ralph Patrick yet."

Sean imagined she was waging an internal battle. Sara was inclined to believe in people. But such faith must be tested after what Nora Ward had just told them. Trinity checked off all three boxes for a killer—means, motive, and opportunity.

"Trinity, we need to ask you a few more questions," Sean said, stepping in, planning to save Sara the trouble of handling this. She glanced at him with a softened expression, which he took as gratitude.

"Whatever you need." At face value, her statement suggested a cooperative spirit free of fear, but the shake in her hand worsened. Austin took the glass from her.

"Just out of curiosity, was your aunt seeing anyone?" One question that was long past due.

"Nope, not even casually."

Sean nodded, pleased that was out of the way. "We spoke to someone who saw you arguing with your aunt in the kitchen. Is that right?" He posed it as a question, though he had no doubt of its validity. Nora Ward struck him as a credible witness despite the fact she had admitted to lying to other people about what she had seen and heard.

"It didn't mean anything," Austin said, stepping in on Trinity's behalf.

"If she could answer..." Sean gestured to the young woman.

Trinity swallowed and paled as if she were about to be sick to her stomach, but she bent over and petted Magnum. Seemingly satisfied, he lay on the floor.

"Trinity, please." Sara touched her forearm. "You can trust us. We'll help you however we can."

His future bride had such a soft heart—one of her greatest qualities—even if it led to disappointment and hurt for her at times. And considering all she'd seen as a cop, the fact she had any faith in humanity was remarkable and a testament to her strong character.

Trinity licked her lips and dipped her head toward Sara. "Yes, I was arguing with my aunt."

"And this was closer to three thirty?" Sara asked. "Not three forty-five, as you originally told us?"

Trinity nodded.

Another person who had initially skirted the truth. And, surely, she had to reason Nora Ward could have come forward and confessed to seeing her. "What was the argument about?"

The young woman told them pretty much the same as Nora Ward had. Then Trinity added, "She wouldn't entertain Juilliard at all. She was being a stubborn mule and dismissive of my dream." Tears fell. "I don't know if I can ever forgive her for that... even now."

That tag-on *even now* struck Sean as cold and bitter. Definite resentment remained, even with her aunt's death. That usually wiped the slate clean, but Darlene's passing was very recent. It was possible that Trinity had killed her aunt and was justifying her actions. Even if in a roundabout way. "Did this argument escalate to physical violence?"

Trinity's mouth gaped open as her eyes widened. "I'd never—" She clamped a hand over her mouth.

Sean wasn't moved by the histrionics. He'd lost count of how many times he'd had a front-row seat to such a performance as a cop. "You never got into a physical altercation with your aunt—ever?"

"No," Trinity said, pouting.

Sean turned to Austin. "Where were you when Trinity was fighting with her aunt?" He used *fighting* instead of *arguing* to see if this would net a reaction. It didn't.

"I was outside having a smoke. I did tell you that," Austin replied calmly.

"You told us you had a cigarette, yes, but you didn't mention a fight was going on between Trinity and her aunt when you were outside." Sean used his words, giving them a twist as if they made up a blade themselves.

Austin's face hardened. "I didn't think it was important. Darlene was very much alive when we left that kitchen. Neither of us had anything to do with what happened to her aunt."

"Their voices were raised enough that you must have heard from outside." Sean was quite sure he must have; Nora Ward had from the neighboring room. He was leading up to another point, an inconsistency or at least an oversight. He needed to lay the foundation first.

"Sure. They were loud. So what?"

Magnum's head lifted, and he eyed Austin with irritability for disturbing his slumber.

"Why didn't you tell us Nora Ward came to check on things?" Sean put his focus on Trinity, who seemed to retreat more and more into the corner. She crossed her arms and rubbed them.

"Trinity," Sara prompted.

"Why would I bring it up?" Trinity cried out. "My fighting with my aunt moments before… *before*…" Trinity collapsed into tears.

"It's all right." Austin wrapped his arm around Trinity and tucked in close to her.

None of this was anywhere close to *all right*. He also noted that Trinity herself had transitioned to using the word *fighting* to describe the situation with her aunt. Was it because he planted that into his questioning, or was the girl finally speaking honestly? "Where were you and your aunt at the time Ms. Ward entered the kitchen?"

"Next to the sink." Trinity sighed, her chest puffing out, then deflating like a balloon. "Aunt Dar had finished touching up the icing and was washing the icing spatula."

"But that's plastic," Sara said quickly. "Isn't it?"

Sean knew why she'd made an issue of that. Nora Ward had mentioned she'd heard something clink against the sink. Plastic wouldn't make that sound.

"Yes." Trinity blinked and furrowed her brow with confusion.

"Was that all that she was cleaning at the time?" Sean didn't know if the answer would be helpful or not. They already had gems to take away from this conversation. Trinity confessed to fighting with her aunt moments before her death, and she had motive and opportunity.

"It's important that you think about your answer," Sara inserted.

"Okay," Trinity dragged out. "There was a spoon."

"Wooden or…" Sean said.

"Silverware."

Sean nodded, that answer possibly checking off the clink that Nora Ward had heard.

"And there was a little glass bowl," Trinity said. "She had to whip up some more icing and used it."

"And during this time, where was the serving knife for the cake?" Sean asked.

"I don't know." Trinity hitched her shoulders. "I assume on the table with the cake. Is that how… what the person used to…?"

Sara pinched her eyes shut and nodded, and Trinity gasped a sob.

Sean was somewhat touched by the scene, as it seemed Trinity was genuinely upset. But he was more focused on the fact she'd just admitted to knowing where to put her hands on the murder weapon. Even if she'd wrapped it up as an assumption. Means and opportunity were also tied up, as was potential for motive. To solidify that, they needed to determine if Trinity was aware of how she would benefit from Darlene's death. "Now that your aunt is dead, what will happen to Locally Baked?"

"I assume I'll get it." Those words appeared to taste bitter as Trinity frowned.

Not exactly the response that Sean had expected. "You don't want it?"

"I told you. My dream is to be a professional ballerina." Trinity met Sean's eyes, no apology.

Her honesty helped her case. "Are you going to sell it, then?"

"I don't have much choice."

"You could hold on to it, take on a management role, or hire people to run the bakery." Sara's facial expression was pained.

A slight smile. "I'm not sure I know enough to do any of that. Aunt Dar said she didn't want to pass her company to someone without a clue of how to keep it going."

"Not talking about you, surely," Sara said. "You just told us she wanted you to take over."

"Yeah, even though it wasn't what I wanted. I have a life to live. And it's different from the one she wanted me to have." She moved closer to Austin, and it was obvious her future as a professional ballerina had a contender.

"You said your aunt didn't want to have her company pass to someone with no experience," Sara began, "but that couldn't have been her reason for not selling to the Bakery Box. Did you get the sense she was talking about someone else who might have wanted to buy the shop?"

Sean looked over at Sara, impressed. Sometimes her logic was based on a sixth sense that bordered on clairvoyance.

"If she was, I don't know who."

Had Sara raised a valid point? Was someone else besides the Bakery Box interested in acquiring Locally Baked? And had that interest led to murder? With Darlene dead, there may be nothing standing in that person's way—whether it be a franchise or an individual. "You mentioned selling the bakery, Trinity. We all know the Bakery Box would take it off your hands today."

"No. I'd never do that," Trinity snapped, offended. "That wasn't what Aunt Dar wanted, and I'll respect her wishes in that regard. But there must be someone in Cotton Spring Falls who shares her vision and would happily take over the business."

"Anyone come to mind?" Sean asked.

Trinity shook her head. "I wasn't around a lot. I've been devoting hours to perfecting my dance."

Sean could understand that. Becoming a ballerina wouldn't be an easy road to take. He could sink low and say that now with her aunt dead she'd have the money for Juilliard, but that struck him as plain cruel. "After you and Austin left the kitchen, you headed to the room for the ceremony? Is that correct?" He was building off what they'd originally been told, making sure that story wasn't going to change.

"That's right."

"Did you see anyone on your way out?" Given the narrow murder window, they must have.

"I don't—" Trinity looked at Austin, her eyes narrowed, then she drew her gaze to Sean.

He perked up. "You did?"

"I think I passed someone, come to think of it. But I was walking with my head down because I was upset about things with my aunt. They were heading toward the kitchen while I was heading through the ballroom to leave for the ceremony."

The cynical part of Sean's mind was stuck on *upset about things with my aunt.* Was it because she'd just stabbed her in the back? He withheld verbalizing the accusation because he was wavering on whether Trinity was a killer. Her grief struck him as genuine, as did her answers.

"Who did you see?" Sara asked as Magnum started snoring at her feet.

"I don't know who," Trinity said. "I'm not even sure if it was a man or woman."

"Because your head was down," Sara said, and Trinity nodded. "Please describe the shoes this person was wearing."

Leave it to Sara to consider that...

"They were black, dressy, and laced." Trinity bobbed her head and jutted out her chin as if to stamp home her conviction.

"A man, then," Sean said, confident in that assessment.

"Ah, not necessarily." Sara shot him a corrective look, and he retreated as if he should have known better. The corners of her mouth softened, then she added, "Some women's dress shoes lace up. Did you notice the size of their feet?"

"No. Sorry."

Sean turned his attention to Austin, who was staring at Trinity's facial profile as she fielded their questions. "Did you see this person? You two were together?" *And, surely, they both weren't walking with their heads down!*

They looked at each other.

Austin eventually said, "Trinity left a few moments before I did."

One other thing they'd failed to mention before… "That left you alone with Darlene, then."

Austin held up a hand. "I had nothing to do with what happened."

"You see how this makes you look suspicious?" Sean was done holding back. He'd done so up until this point out of consideration for Sara, but with all the half-truths stacking up, his self-control was being pushed to its breaking point. "You knew how unhappy Trinity was. You probably would do anything to make her happier."

"No. He didn't." Trinity latched onto Austin's arm in a solid stance of defense.

"You stayed back," Sara chimed in, "after Trinity left. For how long?"

"Just a few seconds."

"And you never saw this person Trinity just mentioned come into the kitchen or on your way through the ballroom?" Sean was seeing so many holes, their stories resembled Swiss cheese.

"No."

"For that matter, why didn't you mention this person before?" Sean piled on another question, and it had Sara laying a hand on his shoulder—her telltale sign to dial down his judgment. But couldn't she see these two were, in the least, guilty of deceit?

"I don't know," Trinity replied.

"I think you do." Sean laid that out with a touch of finesse, not wanting to earn Sara's disapproval.

"I knew if my fight with Aunt Dar got out, people would think I killed her. Police would stop looking for the real killer. Then what?" Trinity sobbed into her hands, and Sara turned to Sean.

The young woman told a similar story as Nora Ward, but Sean also received Sara's unspoken message. She wanted to discuss this conversation in private with him. "Please excuse us," Sean told the young couple and was the first to walk away. Sara was held up as she offered Trinity a hug, which she graciously seemed to accept. But then again, of course, she would. Trinity had someone who believed in her tangled web of stories and excuses. Sara also had to rouse Magnum from dreamland.

Once they were several feet away from Trinity and Austin, Sara turned to Sean. "You're certainly good at playing bad cop."

"Is that a compliment?" He felt like he was tiptoeing across quicksand.

"It absolutely is." She smiled at him, and he felt his shoulders lower. She added, "I just couldn't take on that role with her."

"I understand." And he did. This case touched a little closer to home than any they'd worked while with the Albany PD.

"Trinity said that Darlene didn't want her bakery falling in the hands of a novice, someone with no clue what they were doing."

"I was there and heard that."

She narrowed her eyes and tilted her head. "What do you make of that?"

He had nada and was sure his blank expression would communicate as much.

"Sean," she continued. "That could be a clue. Locally Baked might have had interest from more than one party. She was vocal about refusing the Bakery Box because they're big and impersonal. They represent too much advancement for Cotton Spring Falls. But what if there was someone local who offered to buy Locally Baked? Darlene wasn't getting any younger, and surely, retirement was around the corner for her."

Sean picked up where Sara was headed. "And this person could have been inexperienced at running a bakery?"

"Yep, and angry at Darlene for her high expectations. They might have understood her not selling to the big company but were pushed over the edge when she rejected them, as a fellow resident of the town."

Sean considered, and the first thing to enter his mind was pity for Sara. Trinity and her boyfriend appeared suspect, but Sara eagerly grasped to find alternatives. But he had learned a long time ago to trust her instincts. He was torn but settled on one truth. "We can't rule anyone out just yet."

"Agreed. Oh, look." She indicated a balding man. "That's Ralph Patrick from the Bakery Box. Let's go talk to him."

"Let's." Sean held out his arm for Sara to loop hers through, which she did. He hoped she couldn't see through him, or she'd know that he was quite certain they'd just left Darlene's killer.

Chapter Fifteen

It didn't get any easier for Sara as she watched police officers continuing to make the rounds among their guests. Knowing those closest to her were being questioned about a murder stung. And if one of them was guilty, what did that say about her and Sean's ability to judge a person's character?

As for Trinity Fields, it hurt Sara's heart to consider Darlene's niece as a suspect. Trinity did have motive. She knew Darlene's money would fall to her. The words she'd overheard Darlene say the night of the rehearsal dinner could very well fit with an argument about their main bone of contention.

"I have told you it's not happening" may have been Darlene telling her niece that she wasn't going to fund Juilliard. Then again, it could be several things. And hadn't Darlene said Trinity was off with her boyfriend? Though it was possible she had been there and left. None of this thinking made Sara feel any better. She should just ask Trinity if she had argued with her aunt last night at the restaurant. A part of her feared the answer and how it would affect her objectivity.

But had Trinity killed her aunt? Or had Austin, in a play for approval from his girlfriend?

Last night's words could fit if the rep from the Bakery Box had wormed his way into the kitchen. He could have been there pressuring her on the deadline he'd extended. After all, his presence here told Sara he didn't respect boundaries.

Then there was the potential for an unknown party. Someone interested in buying Darlene's bakery who she had turned away, viewing them as inexperienced. That would be offensive, especially if that person didn't agree. People would go to great lengths to protect their livelihood. *Even further to keep their dreams alive...* That thought had her mind circling back to Trinity.

"Mr. Patrick?" Sean said once he and Sara were a few feet from the man.

Close up, Ralph Patrick looked like he'd had better days. He was flushed like he was overheated, but Sara found the room more on the cool side.

"I am. And you are Sean McKinley and Sara Cain." He passed his gaze over to her and dipped his head at them. He took in Magnum and moved a few steps back.

"Are you afraid of dogs?" she asked him.

"Yeah. I got bit by one as a kid. The experience stayed with me."

Sara pulled back gently on Magnum's leash to prompt him to move closer to her.

"By the way, I'm honored to be here."

She stiffened. "Honored? You weren't invited, Mr. Patrick." She didn't even touch on how a person could be honored to be here considering the circumstances.

Ralph squared his shoulders. "I was."

"If you were, I'd remember." She took pride in her impeccable memory, and she'd reviewed the guest list at least twenty times before she'd stopped counting.

"Here. Look." Ralph slipped his hand under his suit jacket, pulled an envelope from the interior pocket, and gave it to Sean.

Sara shuffled closer to Sean to get a good look. Ralph's name was on an affixed label and not printed directly on the envelope.

"Huh," she said and held out her hand to take it from Sean. "May I?"

He gave it to her, and she slipped the invite out. It looked similar to the ones ordered from the printer, but there were notable differences. For one, the medium. The weight of the paper was too light. The stock much cheaper. She and Sean had decided on recycled paper, thicker and with a notable texture in the grain, and off-white. This one was smooth and bright. Also, the lettering wasn't embossed. The genuine invitations were, their names in a rich purple—a compromise for Sean, keeping her from pink, which was her favorite color. This poor imitation had purple text, but it wasn't the right shade. Overall, it could have been kicked out of someone's home printer.

Sara stiffened. "This invitation is an imitation, Mr. Patrick."

Ralph dabbed his forehead with a few fingers. A nervous tic at being caught?

"Where did you get it? And why are you really here?" Sean asked.

"Why would I have an imitation?"

"Because we didn't invite you," Sara volleyed back.

"And if I were to wager a guess," Sean started, "you wanted to be admitted to our wedding so you could harass Ms. Day further about selling her bakery to the company you work for. But that's just one part of it.

The second is that she wasn't giving you the answer you wanted, so you thought you'd kill her, pick it up from her estate at a steal."

Sara noted Sean left out mention of Trinity's name and was thankful he had.

Sean went on. "Not a horrible place for a murder. Lots of people, affording you a crowd to blend into. But you stand out. Now the police have locked the place down. You must not have considered that would happen."

The flush gone completely from his cheeks, Ralph had paled further with every word that left Sean's mouth. "No, absolutely not." Ralph swallowed roughly, his Adam's apple bulging out like a rat was going down his throat.

Sara waved the invite. "Where did you get this?"

"From Darlene."

Sean narrowed his eyes. "Why on earth would she invite you to our wedding, even go to the trouble of making a fake invitation? From what we hear, she wasn't a fan of you or the company you work for. Why don't you tell us the truth?"

"I am. I swear. Ms. Day said that she was rethinking our proposal and wanted to talk. She said she'd be busy with the wedding today, but we could discuss it here and there. She thought we'd iron things out and come to a fair arrangement."

Sara refused to accept that Darlene had been so presumptuous as to invite Ralph Patrick without first talking to her and Sean. Besides, she wouldn't need to concoct a fake invite. Darlene had clearance to bring in who she needed to help her, and she was also extended the offer of bringing a plus-one. All that aside, Darlene had been strong-willed. Once her mind was made up, it didn't change. "I don't know what sort of fools you take us for—"

Again, Ralph reached into the inside pocket of his jacket. This time he came out with a tri-folded sheet of paper.

"And what's this?" Sean asked, snatching it from Ralph.

"Read it and find out."

Sean unfolded the page and held it for Sara to see as well. Addressed to Ralph Patrick of the Bakery Box, it was a typewritten paragraph with Darlene's signature at the bottom.

Sean read, "'I am giving further consideration to your offer and wish to discuss this with you. As a company that prides itself on being one of the biggest bakery chains in the US, entrusting Locally Baked to your care might not be so terrible. I hope you'll accept the enclosed invitation. You will need it to get past the men at the doors. I will be busy. I'm sure we can come to a fair arrangement throughout the evening.'" He handed the letter to Sara.

She felt peaked. Whoever had sent the letter knew the protocol for gaining entry to the venue.

"See?" Ralph said. "It's as I told you. I assure you I had no ill intentions coming here today. You have to believe me." Ralph laid a hand over his stomach.

Sara bristled, detesting that phrase with a passion. She was a trusting person unless someone told her to be. In those cases, she had to curb her instinctual reaction to consider everything that followed a lie. "We'll be holding on to these, Mr. Patrick."

"If you wish, and I'd be happy to leave if I were permitted."

"No one is leaving until the police say it's okay," Sean said firmly.

Ralph bobbed his head. "I understand. For what it's worth, I'm assuming that Darlene Day was a friend of yours as well." He leveled this at Sara. "I'm very sorry for your loss."

"Thank you." With that, she stepped away from Ralph Patrick, his fake invite and letter in one hand, and Magnum's leash in the other.

"Maybe Darlene was reconsidering the offer from the Bakery Box?" Sean suggested.

"No way." She shared her thinking on that. "Darlene wasn't prone to changing her mind. And even if she was reconsidering, there was no need for a fake invitation. Whoever went to that trouble, I know it wasn't Darlene."

"Right, she'd have no need. He could have just been her escort."

"Exactly." Sara took another look at the letter. There was something off about the signature at quick glance, but a closer inspection revealed what. "This isn't Darlene's signature."

"And how would you know that?"

"Really, Sean?" She smiled at him. "My excellent memory, of course. When I hired her, I signed a contract. She also signed it."

"You think hers looked different than what you're seeing on Mr. Patrick's letter?"

"Not think, I *know*. She finished her Ds with a flourish, and there was a tail that came off the top. Now look at the letter." She held it out for him. "See how her entire name appears more handwritten than an actual signature? And every letter is there, all pristine? Clearly legible?"

"It's almost as if whoever sent this to Ralph Patrick wanted Darlene's name to be easy to read."

"Yep, and I know Darlene's signature was more chicken scratch, making it nearly illegible. She always dropped the last *e* in her first name too. I also know that she preferred blue ink." She pointed out the black ink used for the signature.

"Just because she preferred blue, it doesn't mean she never used black."

"I also have the advantage of remembering the pen she used to sign the contract."

"Do you remember everything?"

She tapped her head. "It's a vault, which you should know by now. But I noticed this particular pen because it was well worn. You could barely tell that it was originally gold-plated. I tried to gift her a new one for helping us out, but she confessed she'd never use it. One reason was it had black ink."

"You're kidding me."

"Nope, and the pen she had meant a lot to her."

"Ridiculous. It's just a pen."

"Not to her. It was the one she used when signing the lease on the building for Locally Baked. She said it always brought her luck." Sara frowned at the last sentiment, though a pen could hardly be blamed for murder. *Unless it was used as a weapon*, the thought fired through.

"Well, whatever's going on, we'll figure it out, Sara. We always do."

"You will figure what out, Mr. McKinley?" It was Ryan Doyle, and his partner was standing at his left shoulder.

Magnum sniffed at Ryan's pant leg, snorted, and dropped to the floor, lying on his side. It was a comical move Sara had witnessed on many occasions. It was like he was a puppet whose strings had been cut.

"Has anyone ever told you it's not polite to eavesdrop?" Sean responded.

"Yes, well, during an open murder investigation, that is moot. What trouble are you two getting yourselves into now?"

"Just talking with our guests," Sean said.

Ryan made a show of looking around. "Is the one you're with now invisible?"

Sara's hackles rose, unsure when he'd become such a pompous bleep-bleep-bleep. "Ryan, you're being insufferable and rude, and—"

"I am the detective in charge of finding out what happened to Darlene Day and, as far as I'm concerned, you're still a suspect."

"How is that even possible?" Sean snapped.

Sara put a hand on Sean's arm. Lashing out wouldn't quell Ryan's attitude. It was obviously born of prejudice and male pride. "I was in the bridal suite—with witnesses—at the time Darlene was stabbed. As we've been over."

"*And* as I made clear, your witnesses comprise of your mother and two closest friends. I'm sure they'd say anything to protect you."

"And my motive would be what, exactly?" she shoved back. "Why would *I* kill Darlene Day?"

Louise rolled her eyes.

"Even your partner doesn't buy it, Ryan," Sean said, nudging his head toward Louise. He must have caught her reaction too.

"Detective Doyle," he corrected, bristling.

"Mr. McKinley's right," Louise said, her voice small, but she stepped forward to assert herself. "There's no evidence against Sara or any in her party. They were just the unfortunate ones who were present when Ms. Day passed."

A pulse tapped in Ryan's cheeks, and they blushed bright red. Sara knew the look well. He was livid, but he'd tamp it down and blow up later.

"What do you have there?" Ryan pointed at the paperwork in Sara's hand.

"It's none of your business," Sean stepped in.

"It is if it's related to the investigation."

"Why would it be?" Sara countered, not a lie, just a vague misdirection.

"Uh-huh. Well, Mr. McKinley and Ms. Cain, if I get the feeling just one more time that you are sticking your nose into this investigation, I will have you arrested." He made firm eye contact with Sara. "And don't doubt me on that. I suggest you go over to your parents and stay with them."

Sara followed the direction of Ryan's finger that pointed toward Jeannie and Leon. There was a woman standing beside her mother she didn't recognize. *Someone's plus-one?*

"Think about your next moves carefully," Ryan threatened and walked away with Louise trailing. She mouthed an apology as she passed Sara.

"If he wasn't a cop…" Sean was seething and had a hand formed into a fist.

Sara laid her hand over it. "Violence solves nothing."

He softened under her touch and faced her. "What would I do without you?"

"Get yourself into a heap of trouble."

"Huh. I think I do that quite well by your side." He laughed.

"Hey." She shoved his shoulder, but the moment of levity only lasted a few seconds. The gloom overhead that someone—a person she knew, no less—had died in this building, on her and Sean's wedding day, weighed heavily. She lifted Ralph's invitation and the letter. "We need to ask who would go to such lengths to get Ralph Patrick here—and why."

"*Who* seems to be an easy one."

"The killer," they said in unison.

"Not that we have a name," he added.

And without that first piece of the puzzle, discovering motive would be near impossible.

Chapter Sixteen

Sean was reconsidering his initial theory of the killer staying out of fear of being noticed. He or she could have been someone who snuck their way into the venue. "It's apparent the security isn't as tight as we had hoped."

Sara shook her head. "It's quite unsettling. First, Desiree gets in, and now Mr. Patrick. He had an invitation, but it was a poor imitation."

"Even if they missed that, the security guards were to compare the invites to a master list."

"About that… The sender of the invite and the letter knew about the protocol for getting into the venue. Remember the letter? The sender told Mr. Patrick he'd need the invite."

Sean sighed. "Could be anyone, be it guest, employee, or well-informed wedding crasher."

The disappointment in Sara's eyes threatened to capsize him, but he understood why she felt that way. The day was hardly recognizable as the one they had planned. All that spoke to what could have been was the decorated hall, the mingling guests, and the tuxedo he still wore. It was frustrating that all their preventive steps to ensure the venue was secure had been ineffective. Even the backgrounds they had Jimmy pull on the assigned security team meant nothing—apparently. What if someone was a last-minute replacement? Were any of the guards working in cahoots with Darlene Day's killer? It wasn't like Jimmy had done a deep dive into the guards' personal lives. "What if we are looking at someone on the security team?"

"If we're going there, Sean, we should consider anyone working here today."

"The caterers," he volleyed back.

"Yep. And those shoes Trinity described could have belonged to a security guard or someone with Belle Catering. We can't narrow it down to just men, either."

"We also can't overlook that the person who sent that forged invite to Ralph Patrick must have had at least a peek at an original one." It felt like every time one of them opened their mouth, the situation became more insurmountable.

"Right… So we're back to someone that we invited being a criminal."

He wasn't going to correct her by saying *killer*. "I'm sorry, sweetheart, but no matter how we dissect this, I'm saddened to say that must hold truth."

"Then let's recap. Darlene was killed within a ten-minute window—" She stopped talking when their gazes met.

His eyes must have given him away.

Ten minutes, according to Trinity and her boyfriend. They hadn't exactly been fully cleared as suspects in his mind.

"I can read you, Sean. I'm going by what we've been told. Not just from Trinity and Austin, but also Nora Ward. Remember, she told us she saw Darlene in the kitchen near the sink with Trinity… away from the murder weapon."

He could point out going the distance from the sink to the cake knife on the counter would have taken no time at all, but Sara had to know that. He'd pick things up from a different direction. "Austin admits he didn't leave the kitchen with Trinity, rather a bit after her. Could he have a reason to kill Ms. Day?"

"I don't know him enough to say. Even if he didn't agree with the fact Darlene wasn't letting Trinity go to Juilliard, how would killing Darlene benefit him?"

"Love makes people do crazy things."

"That, I agree with." Sara smiled at him and touched his upper arm. He put his hand over hers.

The entire sordid mess was disheartening, but sinking into misery wouldn't get them anywhere closer to Darlene Day's killer. They had to think like a killer. Just acknowledging that had a discrepancy popping up for him. "The murder method appears to have been in the moment, rash, using a weapon at hand. But how does that reconcile with the forethought that must have gone into getting Ralph Patrick in attendance? That indicates he may have been intended to be a patsy."

"Huh, that's a very interesting thought."

"Well, from the looks of you two, I should interrupt." Jimmy had sidled up next to Sean so quietly that he hadn't even noticed until he spoke. But that was his light-footed former sergeant. "And how's our little friend doing?" He pulled a treat from a pocket and bent down and handed it to Magnum. The beagle bit down and swallowed. Magnum the Hoover pup. The hound eyed Jimmy for another and howled. Several people turned to them, smiles on their faces, despite the otherwise somber atmosphere. Leave it to a dog to elevate people's moods.

"Yes, buddy, I know, I know." Jimmy took a second treat from his pocket and gifted it to Magnum who, like the Great Houdini, pulled a disappearing trick. "Not even sure he tastes them," Jimmy said.

"I can't see how he would." Sean shook his head.

"All right, enough dancing around. When I came over here, you two were deep in conversation, your heads angled together. I recognize that look. I saw it a lot when you were with Albany PD and working a case. You're still not letting this go, are you?"

"How can we, Jimmy?" Sara said.

"Well, again, I shall say it. Watch your backs."

"Speaking of, there's something you should both know. Maybe I should have said before now. But I happened overhear Doyle and Farmer talking earlier. Farmer thought he was being a little hard on us. Doyle placed the blame for that on the sergeant."

"Hugh Thornton, our MC? And you just thought to share this now?" Sara's mouth set in a grimace.

"What can I say? There's been a lot going on since I heard this."

"We need to talk to him, then, sort all this out," Sara said with conviction.

"Yeah, I don't think that's a good idea." This from Jimmy.

Sara turned to him. "You're right. It might be best if you spoke to him. You know, sergeant to sergeant."

"Me? I don't even know the guy."

"You've met," Sara shot back.

"Quite a leap to *knowing* the guy," Jimmy pointed out.

Sara hitched her shoulders. "Fair enough, but you could have a talk with him, feel out where he's coming from."

"I can tell you right now. He wants everything about this investigation to be aboveboard. You can be certain his superiors will take a look at how this one is handled. With him being a guest—master of ceremonies, at that— he's very close to this."

Sara let out a deep sigh.

"Suppose that holds water," Sean admitted. "Maybe we leave him alone."

"Should we, though?" Sara asked. "He could have killed Darlene. He's one of the few here who didn't agree with her holding back progress in Cotton Spring Falls."

Sean leveled his gaze at her. "You really believe your former sergeant committed murder?" Her implication surprised him, as she had been so resistant to believing anyone here had. "Because unless you're fully convinced, I say leave it, like Jimmy. No good can come of it."

Sara seemed to give it some thought. "Okay."

"But, Jimmy, Sara and I could use your help." Sean stood taller, trying to communicate confidence in his former sergeant's cooperation. Maybe if that was what he put out, he'd get it in return.

"And why would I want to do that? I still have a job I need to keep."

"You never have to worry about money as long as we're around," Sean assured him. "We'll always have your back."

"I might need to hold you to that."

Sean and Sara smiled at each other, then Jimmy.

He shook his head. "I really need to learn to say no to you two."

The hardened sergeant had a soft spot for them, and Sean would use it to their advantage. "There's that background report we talked about before."

"Austin Palmer?"

"Yep, but we also have some concerns about the security team on the premises," Sean said.

"I checked them all. No criminal records, nothing that flagged."

"Which we know, but somehow at least two people got in who shouldn't have. You looked into the ones assigned in advance, but is it possible someone stepped in at the last minute?" he asked.

"The owner of the security company was to let me know if that was going to be the case, but I mean, everyone is just human. Who got admitted who shouldn't have?"

"A reporter from the *New York Times* and Ralph Patrick from the Bakery Box," Sara put in.

"The people after Day's bakery?"

"The very ones."

"I can talk to the guards, see what they have to say on the matter."

"Sean and I were thinking for the reporter, she could have paid a bribe. Ralph Patrick got in with a fake invite that someone sent him."

Jimmy's eyes narrowed. "What is that now?"

Sean filled him in on the invite and letter.

"That sounds planned."

"What Sara and I thought."

"All right, well, I'll see what I can find out around here. As for the background, I'm not sure I'll be able to get out to do that. I would call the station and ask someone to pull it, but I don't want to rope anyone else into this circus."

"We understand," Sean said, speaking for himself and Sara. Answering on behalf of them as a couple felt incredible. For years, he didn't think he and Sara would ever get together.

"Well, it looks like this little guy could do with a wee walkabout, so I'll take him off your hands." Jimmy held out his hand to take the leash from Sean.

"Thanks." There was no need to remind Jimmy he'd been out recently.

"Hey, don't mention it. I plan to use the little guy. He has a way of getting people to talk." Jimmy dipped his head and headed for the ballroom's exit.

"Wonder how he's going to escape with Ryan, his partner, and other CSFPD officers floating around," Sara said.

"That's the thing with Jimmy. You can never underestimate the man." As he watched Jimmy get closer to freedom, Sean wished he and Sara were going with him. But they were stuck in this room—at least for now. They were also without their usual assets in such an investigation—no trace evidence to examine or phone records, to start. They were approaching this with their hands tied behind their backs and blindfolds over their eyes. He didn't much care for either.

Chapter Seventeen

Sara grappled with the multitude of potential suspects. But why kill Darlene here, today? Was there a grander purpose at play, or was it simply to blend into the crowd? She hated to consider it might even be a personal affront to her and Sean, a means of ruining their wedding as well as eliminating Darlene. Who present would want to do both?

Her life as a homicide detective taught her that killers were often selfish and egotistical creatures. They also made justifications for their actions. It likely applied to the person who had stabbed Darlene in the back. But there was another trait that applied to most killers. Most were conniving, whether or not the act was planned. It was possible the murder hadn't been as opportunistic as it appeared. Especially if it somehow involved getting Ralph Patrick in attendance. "Sean, just thinking… The only thing that appears opportunistic is the cake knife, but then there's the fact that someone—most likely the killer—wanted Ralph Patrick here."

"Which we touched on. It seems straightforward to me that the killer wants us to think that Ralph Patrick put the knife in Darlene's back."

"Yes, and that would indicate her murder was orchestrated. This also means it's likely the killer had a tenuous relationship with Darlene long before today."

"I'm on board with that."

"And it seems it was public knowledge that Darlene refused any offers from the Bakery Box."

"Right, which doesn't narrow things down for us."

"Not entirely. Everyone knows everyone else's business in Cotton Spring Falls whether they want to or not."

"Eavesdropping and spying are the staples around here."

She smiled. "Pretty much. The townspeople pride themselves on being in the know. And the letter that accompanied the invite only proves the killer knew about the offer on the table. They'd also need to know what our invites looked like to even attempt imitating them. But circling back to where I started. The cake knife being at hand doesn't reconcile with the premeditation required to get Patrick in attendance."

"Still following."

"Further, I think the knife and how it was used might be a message." Her heart sped up as a theory crystalized into form.

"She was stabbed in the back," Sean said slowly.

"Returning to what I said about the killer having a history with Darlene, I think we're looking for someone who felt like Darlene Day had stabbed them in the back. Only they repaid the favor in the literal sense."

Sean frowned, and she sensed what he was thinking.

"Sean, I realize this doesn't eliminate Trinity, with their disagreement about her future, but I also ask that you keep an open mind."

"Always." He pecked a kiss to her forehead, and the two of them pulled apart as Jeannie came over.

The woman who had been with her was walking in the opposite direction. With Sara's mind on the conversation with Sean, she only now noticed her outfit. She was dressed in white from top to bottom, except for her shoes, which were flat and black with laces. She must have been with the catering company.

"Sara, everyone is growing restless and uneasy," Jeannie said. "Well, actually, past that point, but don't you think we could have the caterers roll out something for people to eat?"

Since that woman was heading toward the doors, it seemed her mother might have already relayed the direction for her to do just that. But Sara agreed. "It has been hours." Sara said this while looking at Sean, despite the response being elicited by her mother's concern. "What can we put out, though?"

Jeannie said, "I was just talking to Vanessa and—"

"Vanessa?" Sara angled her head. "I'm not familiar with her."

"Vanessa Brady. She's new to town and recently divorced from her husband of ten years. Guess she found out he was sleeping with his secretary. The sad cliché in action."

"I don't remember that name from the guest list."

"That's because she isn't a guest, Sara. She's with Belle Catering."

That confirmed Sara's suspicion about her reason for being here. Sara was thinking how she and Sean had discussed that security was vetted, but had Jimmy been as thorough when it came to the catering company? They hadn't asked him about that. "Do you know Vanessa well?"

"As I said, she's new to town. Just moved in a couple of months ago."

That was long enough to get a feel for the townspeople—who was who and the latest scuttlebutt. Unlike some small towns, Cotton Spring Falls was mostly open to newcomers. That was, unless they were trying to change the place. "And how is she liking it? Is she fitting in all right?"

"Yes, Sara, as far as I know. But going back to your question and the matter of feeding your guests, the easiest thing to hand out would be the cake." Jeannie's body was rigid, and it obviously pained her to suggest it.

Sara's heart sank. The cake that she had gone to great pains with Darlene to make just right. The same cake that had occupied Darlene's last moments alive. But this day was already ruined, so really, what was one confection on top of that? It should have been a no-brainer response, but she couldn't get herself to speak.

"Sara?" Sean prompted her and cupped her elbow. "It's up to you."

"Yeah, I mean, why not?" Her logic knew there would be other cakes, but this was to have been *the* cake to mark her big day. But there may be a compromise she could make... "Actually, if the police allow us to feed people, just have the backup cakes brought out." There was *the* cake, which was the tiered one, and then two rectangular ones to compensate for the number of people here. "Darlene would have likely kept them in the fridge."

"I'll make sure that happens. That's if the police will let the catering staff into the kitchen where Darlene was..." Jeannie rubbed her throat. "Vanessa said they wouldn't earlier."

Because it's a crime scene... "Just clear it past Ryan," Sara called out to her mother, who was already on the move. "This day is going from bad to worse with every passing minute." She said it just loud enough for Sean to hear.

"I know you're disappointed, sweetheart. So am I."

She looked at him, and when their gazes met, she felt better. She still had Sean. That was what really mattered. And with her personal disappointments under control, her mind was back on the case. "Vanessa Brady. New to town, but she'd have known Darlene quite well. Newcomers can't help but know her. She was involved in everything."

"Vanessa could be a recluse."

"I don't think that's permitted in Cotton Spring Falls."

"Really?"

"You'd have no reason to know, but there is an actual committee whose sole purpose is to welcome new people."

"Wow. Really?"

She smiled at how Sean was sounding like a record on repeat. "*Really.* My mother is part of it, but Darlene headed it up."

"And what do they do exactly?"

"Two to three members visit any newcomer at their home, bringing a pie of some sort and usually a casserole."

"Definitely in the backwoods here. That would never happen in the city. You can live beside someone for years and never learn their name."

"And which is sadder?" She took slight offense at the term *backwoods* as if it were derogatory.

"Not arguing with you on that point. More places should be like Cotton Spring Falls."

"Yeah, if only such an idyllic little town didn't house a murderer." The bitter truth of that burrowed deep, and the chills only grew into goose bumps when an announcement was made that cake was coming out.

Chapter Eighteen

Jimmy certainly didn't have a memory like Sara. His was more sieve than retainer, but he got along most of the time. Usually all it took was a prompt for his thoughts to click into place. But what he wouldn't give to have a mind as sharp as Sara's. Then he'd be able to say in the affirmative that every security guard's face was familiar. He'd just recall it from having seen their background reports. But it didn't work like that for him.

Officers permitted him and Magnum to leave the ballroom with explicit instructions they weren't to be long. Two security guys were posted inside the front doors, likely being removed from their position outside and replaced with officers from the Cotton Spring Falls PD. It was surprising they weren't being treated as criminals and corralled with everyone else in the ballroom. Ryan What's-His-Face and his partner must not have considered them a threat. And that was just one area where the young detective took a false step. The other was he seemed so blinded by jealousy, he couldn't approach the investigation with a clear head. Even Jimmy could see from the brief interactions he'd witnessed that

Ryan had a thing for Sara. And as soon as any personal feelings were pulled into a case, it fell apart. There was no objectivity or clear vision.

"Hey ya, fellas. How are ya doing?" Jimmy asked the guards once he reached them. He'd already spoken with them when he'd requested that they lock the place down—long before Detectives Doyle and Farmer had even shown up.

"As good as expected," the bigger of the two said.

Again, the guy's name… It had flown right out of Jimmy's head. "The day's certainly taken an unexpected turn."

"Say that again," the other one chirped in.

"So it's you two on the front doors and…" Jimmy was playing it up as if he were stupid, but he knew there was also one guy posted on the rear door and another on the side.

"It's me and Doug Sanders here, Bobby McCall at the rear, and Zeke Hale on the side door," the bigger guy said.

The names all sounded familiar, but he couldn't be sure. "And your name? I don't remember off the top."

"Garrett Golden."

"And all of you were scheduled to come here today, no last-minute substitutions?"

Golden shook his head. "I wish I could say, but we just go to our assigned posts and get to work."

"You don't know? No meeting beforehand?" This seemed like a huge hole in security measures, and Jimmy wasn't impressed.

"We may have dropped the ball there."

May have? The security company certainly wouldn't be getting a glowing online review.

"I met the one guy before we got going. Think he was watching the side door. I swear he said his name was Joe Mercer, though," Sanders said.

Jimmy wasn't senile and knew that was a different name than the one Golden had just provided. "You just met? You don't know each other?"

Golden and Sanders looked at each other and shook their heads.

"We don't know everyone with the company," Sanders said.

Strange... "I do have another question for you both."

"Whatever you need, Mr. Voigt," Sanders said.

"Before either of you let anyone in, you checked their invites, correct?"

"Of course." Golden peacocked his stance.

Did he take offense to Jimmy questioning his work ethic or did he have something to hide? "All right, well, that's good. And you've been cross-checking the invites with the list you were provided?"

Both men looked at each other.

"You cross-referenced?" Jimmy pressed.

"We did, but we allowed one man in who had an invite but wasn't on the list," Sanders said. "I made a note of his name. Ralph Patrick."

Jimmy knew from Sara and Sean that was the man with the Bakery Box, the one with the fake invitation. "Did someone tell you to do this? Did you clear his admission past anyone?" Jimmy asked, but he knew they certainly hadn't approached him.

"With a Darlene Day." Golden pointed at a scrawled name next to Patrick's.

"Darlene Day, the murder vic—"

"Jimmy Voigt." A man dragged out his name. "I thought you were taking the dog out to do its business, but it seems you're just as bad as Sean and Sara and are meddling in my investigation."

Jimmy took a measured breath and turned to face Detective Doyle. He didn't look old enough to have a badge, let alone a gold shield. What was with cops getting younger and younger these days? Or was it more a reflection on him and how the years had passed far too quickly? "Nope. I am just taking the little fella out. Just stopped to shoot the breeze for a minute."

"Huh. Didn't sound like that to me." Doyle crossed his arms. "I would have thought you'd be coming back in by this point."

"Yeah? Well, you thought wrong. If you'll excuse me, gentlemen." Jimmy pushed forward and stepped outside with Magnum. Thankfully, Doyle read his energy and stayed inside.

But curse Doyle. Just before he had turned up, Jimmy was on the verge of getting somewhere. Golden had said Darlene Day told them to allow Ralph Patrick inside. That made zero sense. For one, Day would have been busy with her work in the kitchen and not loitering by the front door. Two, from all accounts, Day didn't even like Ralph Patrick, as he represented the Bakery Box. Jimmy would place a bet that even if he'd been able to show the guards a picture of Day, she wouldn't be the woman they'd encountered. That left a mystery to solve—if not Darlene Day, who?

The obvious answer was it must have been whoever had invited Patrick and wrote that letter pretending it was from Darlene—was it one and the same *and* the killer? If only Jimmy could reach inside their brains and pull out her picture. But by all accounts, there was a high probability that a woman had plunged that knife into Darlene Day's back. Could it have been her niece, Trinity Fields? From what he'd gathered, she had motive.

There was also the concern that arose with the two sets of names for the guard on the side door—Zeke Hale and Joe Mercer. Were any of the guards to be trusted? They'd not just dropped the ball by letting Ralph Patrick through but also the reporter. Jimmy hadn't even had a chance to ask about her. It seemed the security guys were ignoring protocol and doing whatever they liked. In the least, it seemed one of them was favorable to a bribe. But was that as far as their shortcomings went, or was one of them also in on the plan to kill Darlene Day?

Chapter Nineteen

Vanessa from Belle Catering was at a table on one side of the ballroom cutting up the cake and distributing it to the wedding guests, most of whom were in line to be served. It was such a horrible thing to witness. Sara felt for them as much as for herself and Sean—and their cake. By the time it was originally going to be dished out, people should have been dancing and joyful. She'd have been Mrs. Cain-McKinley for a few hours already. Also, she would have been the first to slice into the tiered cake and serve up a piece to Sean... using the same knife that ended up in Darlene's back. Then a thought hit. "Sean, the cake knife ended up in Darlene's back, so what is Vanessa using to cut the cake?" Maybe this whole thing was moot. It could have been a regular old knife plucked from the utensil drawer in the community center. Though, from what she knew, they didn't stock the place with much of anything. She was told they'd need to bring in anything they'd need.

Sara led the way across the ballroom, weaving through the guests. Most of them offered her and Sean their sympathies. They thanked people for their kind words as they continued making forward progress.

She and Sean cut the line and beelined to Vanessa. She smiled at them. While she had never met them, Sara suspected that her mother had pointed out who they were. And if she hadn't, someone would have. She imagined it went something like, *"There's the poor bride and groom…"*

"Ms. Brady, is it?" Sara said, and the woman handed the plate she'd just loaded with a piece of cake to Gertie Smith, someone she and Sean still needed to talk to. But it would have to wait.

"You can call me Vanessa," the woman said and loaded another plate with cake. She extended this one to Sara.

She waved her off. "No, thank you."

Sean rejected it as well, but Sara's mind was on what Vanessa was using to cut the cake. Sara could plainly see that it was an actual cake serving knife. She pointed at it. "Where did you get that?"

"The kitchen." Vanessa looked from Sara to Sean, her eyebrows quirked up at Sara's question.

"Where precisely?" Sara asked.

"It was on the drying rack in the sink."

Nora Ward had heard something *clink* against the stainless steel of the sink when Darlene was doing dishes. But why would Darlene be washing the serving knife when it hadn't been used yet? On the surface, this didn't make any sense. They were missing some pieces of the puzzle. "Okay, thanks." Sara smiled at her and turned to walk away.

Sean kept close to her side. "What's going through that beautiful head of yours?"

"It just isn't making any sense." She told him about her thoughts.

"Okay, well, Darlene may have brought two for some reason."

"I guess. We could ask Trinity to see if she knows. Otherwise, it would be further evidence of premeditation. First, getting Ralph Patrick here. Two, bringing the murder weapon along with them."

"It's possible, but I'm still not sure where that gets us."

"We need in that kitchen again to have a good look around."

"That's if we can talk our way past Officer Simms." Sean hitched his shoulders.

"Worth trying. But Sean." She stopped walking and faced him. "We made sure the security personnel checked out and the catering company itself, but what about its employees? One of them could have easily brought in a serving knife—known to others or secreted away."

"Possible, I guess. I don't know if Jimmy dug deep on them."

"I understand they wouldn't strike as much of a potential threat as those watching the entrance points, but we might do best to reconsider. It's obvious whoever killed Darlene was in the kitchen anyway."

"In the least to kill her. But as your mom told us, Vanessa said the catering staff wasn't permitted into the kitchen where Darlene was murdered."

"Doesn't mean one of them hadn't *happened* to go in anyway."

"Someone with the intent to murder."

"Exactly. And no one would question them. They are all dressed in white, easily identifiable as working with Belle Catering."

"We'll need to talk to all of them, see where it gets us."

"It was so much easier when we were officially responsible for murder investigations. We had resources at our fingertips. We could pull backgrounds. In this case, we don't even have access to Darlene's phone."

"Already thought that, and we don't know whether the killer took it or left it behind."

"If we still had our badges, we would know. And even if we couldn't put our hands on the phone, we could request her records."

"Yes, well, we have what we have."

"And what's that?" The question came out, birthed from frustration.

"Each other, and that's more than enough."

"Aw, Sean, there's yet another reason I want to marry you."

"Besides my good looks and charm?"

"Yes, besides those." She touched his cheek. "Your confidence."

"Let's go see what it nets us, shall we?"

They walked toward the kitchen doors that came off the ballroom. Officers were scattered around the room, their notepads still in hand as they asked their questions and recorded answers. What was taking them so long was beyond Sara's comprehension, but she supposed they wanted to be thorough. Something beyond a guest list that she and Sean could have easily provided. She wondered if Ryan and his partner suspected a wedding crasher of the murder. Honestly, it was what Sara preferred the result would be. To think she or Sean was a poor judge of character was more upsetting. "Actually," she said, "I just had an idea that might help us…" She hurried back to Vanessa and secured a piece of cake.

"Change your mind?" Sean asked her.

"It's not for me." She slightly dipped her head toward Officer Simms, who was standing at the entrance to the kitchen, his arms crossed over his torso.

"Sara. Sean."

"This is for you." Sara smiled at him as she handed over the cake and a fork.

"Oh, you're lifesavers." Gus happily took the offering and started shoveling forkfuls of cake into his mouth.

Soft, sweet, succulent… Sara thought of how it had tasted when she'd approved it with Darlene. Her stomach rumbled, but she knew better than to put food in there right now.

"We were hoping to just grab something from the kitchen," Sara said, hoping she was pulling off damsel in distress.

"I'm sorry, but I can't let you in there. Doyle would have my hide." Gus put more cake into his mouth.

"We won't be long."

"I dunno. What do you need?"

Sara's heart bumped off rhythm. She was making all this up as she went along.

"Uh-huh, as I thought. You can't be investigatin' this, Sara." Gus swept the fork around the plate, scooping up every trace of icing he could.

"I'm not. We're not. Just five minutes. Please."

Gus took a deep breath that had his barrel chest expanding. His gaze cut across the room, and Sara followed the direction of it straight to Ryan, who was talking with one of her best friends, Valerie Morgan. He really was relentless.

"Just five minutes. Please," she repeated, beseeching him.

"Fine. Be quick."

Gus barely stepped aside enough to allow them room to get by.

They slipped inside the kitchen, and Sean turned to her.

"Now what, Sara?"

"That I don't know." Her eyes drifted to where the tiered cake had been, but it was gone. She wondered where it had ended up. "This is the scene of the murder, so let's approach it like one."

"Speaking of, did crime scene investigators just fly through here?"

"It doesn't seem like they took much time, does it?"

"Not really. But it is a rather small space."

Sara left Sean's side and went over to where Magnum had sniffed out the feather and ducked down. It was gone, likely collected by crime scene investigators. Score one for them. "The feather is gone, so we can assume it was collected as evidence."

"Right. And yet another oddity. The killer invites a patsy, packs a second serving knife—for a backup contingency—and they are a… bird." The skin around Sean's eyes crinkled with his smile.

She shook her head. "I doubt the latter bit. But what are we missing…?" She put her hands on her hips and tapped an index finger against herself. There was something on the tip of her mind, but it wasn't coming into focus. She went over to the sink. A small plate and a fork were on the drying rack, along with a small bowl and a spatula—likely what was used to touch up the icing. The investigators must not have found any of this worth their attention.

If Vanessa Brady was to be believed, this was where she'd have found the serving knife. But hadn't Trinity told them it was near the cake? No, she hadn't been certain. Her recollection must have been taking a bit of a hit from exhaustion. Amid all these thoughts, Sara's mind churned up Darlene's last word again. *Icing.*

If only she could have gotten out more, or just skipped the vague clue and named her killer. Speaking of… "Sean, maybe we're wrong about the killer having a long-standing rivalry with Darlene. She might not have told me her killer's name because she didn't know it."

"Or she never saw them coming."

"Right," she dragged this out. "Which is probably more likely, considering everything. So Darlene was in the kitchen fixing up the icing, then had an argument with Trinity. She and Austin left, and the killer came in, presumably when Darlene had walked over to the cake—near where we found the pool of blood—and just stabbed her in the back? Seemingly out of the blue?"

"I think we can both agree there must have been a history between Darlene and her killer. As for why Darlene chose to say 'icing' instead of her killer's name, I don't know."

Sara had a thought. What if it had been her niece, and Darlene's silence was a last act to protect the girl? But why if she had stabbed her? Surely, that would be enough to destroy any nurturing tendency Darlene would feel for her niece. In fact, this consideration strongly suggested Trinity Fields's innocence. Still, why say *icing*?

"Don't forget that when the killer struck, they also may have left a piece of themselves behind. The feather."

She narrowed her eyes, not missing the way he'd phrased things. "Let it go. The killer isn't a bird," she said drily, and he smiled. "It could have fallen out of a pocket."

"Who carries around feathers?"

"I suspect more people than you might imagine." She tapped a hand against her thigh, deep in concentration. "Feathers, feathers…" Maybe if she repeated it enough, something would click into place. "Some might think they represent something, like a loved one visiting. I'm quite sure they have importance for aboriginal people."

"Without pigeon-holing the investigation, no pun intended, and making this about race, are any people of that background present? Man, it doesn't feel right to ask that."

"It's not even necessary. I suppose anyone who is superstitious might place importance in feathers."

"Any of the guests fit that description?"

"Sadly, yes. Gertie Smith, Molly's best friend. Gertie owns a new-age shop on the main street. Crystals, talismans, amulets, gemstones, tarot cards, you name it."

"And she's someone who likes feathers?"

Sara had spoken little with Gertie in the last couple of years, but she remembered she used to wear a necklace with a bead and feathers. "Yes. Used to, anyway."

"And didn't you say earlier that she opposed Darlene's stand on keeping Cotton Spring Falls just as it is?"

"Yep."

"She just moved up our suspect list, but if you want to still have a look around here, I suggest we do that before we get kicked out."

Sara nodded, tamping down the hurt that came with thinking Gertie was a killer. The woman seemed to have such a calm spirit—for the most part. Sara had seen her lose her temper in the past, though, and it hadn't been pretty. But what motive would she have to kill Darlene Day? Was it just their difference of opinion on the town's future?

Chapter Twenty

Sean was uncomfortable in this room, and it wasn't because a woman had been stabbed here. Rather, he preferred to remain a free man to live his life with the woman he loved. If Doyle found out that he and Sara were still meddling, Sean wasn't counting on the detective's good graces to keep him out of jail. Sara might be given a pass, but not him.

Sara was near where she had found the feather, opening up the cabinet in the island above it. "Nothing in there." She moved on to the next.

Sean opened drawers and cupboards, doing so quietly. He had no idea what he was looking for, but sometimes that was when the best clues revealed themselves. He made the rounds in a quick fashion and found himself in the walk-in pantry. Nothing of note beyond the bottles of red wine as backup stock they had brought in for the reception.

Next, he opened the double doors on the sub-zero fridge. Quite a nice appliance for a community center in a small town. No expense spared there.

The shelves weren't full in this one. The catering staff must have loaded up the fridge in the other kitchen with all the hors d'oeuvres, ingredients for the night's meals, bottles of champagne and white wine.

There was one thing in the fridge that shouted out to him, though. It was a small plastic container. Sean pulled it out and cracked the lid. A portion of their wedding cake, but there was a chunk missing from it.

Sean put together what this might mean. "Sara," he said to her, and motioned her over and shared his find.

"Darlene must have gotten munchy," she said.

"What I was thinking too. It also accounts for the plate and fork near the sink. Possibly the serving knife Vanessa found next to the sink too."

Sara opened the door to the walk-in freezer and stepped back with a gasp.

"What is—" But he didn't need to finish his question. Their tiered cake had been moved to the freezer. *It's on ice, just like our marriage…* The thought would have been humorous if it wasn't so sad and true. "It will keep better than sitting around for who knows how long." He knew the second the words left his mouth that he'd made a faux pas. "I didn't mean that the way it came out."

"No, you did, Sean. And you're right. Who knows when we'll get married now."

"Come here." Sean opened his arms, and she stepped into them and wrapped hers around him. He tapped a kiss on her forehead. "We'll get married as soon as we can get out of here."

"But everyone we love is in that other room."

"Not to sound selfish, Sara, but it's you and I that really count here. Those who love us will understand, and we could hold a huge party after."

"You're suggesting we elope?" She drew back.

"It's not completely illogical. You must admit today's been a little insane."

"Yes, and an anomaly. Why do I have to give up my dream wedding, Sean?"

"That's here in a community center in Cotton Spring Falls?"

"It's not this building. It's where my loved ones are, my family and yours."

His aunt Gwen, the only blood relative he had left. He should have checked in with her to see how she was handling all this.

Sara added, "We will wait until the time is right. Please promise me that."

He didn't want to wait a second longer to marry her, but it felt like their future was dangling by a thread and it was in danger of snapping. "I'd do anything for you. If you want to wait, we'll wait."

"I don't want to wait. Well, not really, but I don't think we have any other choice. I want my family to be a part of this. Don't you want that?"

Family… That was a tough one to process. He'd love for his father to have been here, to witness him marry his soulmate, but he'd died when Sean was seventeen. And he knew better than to expect his mother to come. He hadn't seen a trace of her since she'd left him as a toddler for his father to raise alone. Maybe one day, he'd track her down. *Maybe.* After all, he'd gotten along quite well without her in his life up to this point, and there was nothing she could say that would make him forgive her for all the hurt she'd caused. And not just because of his own pain but what he'd witnessed in his father's eyes when he didn't think Sean was looking. "I do."

"I thought we were going to wait." She flickered a smile, and it took Sean a few seconds to stitch together the humor.

"Yes, we will wait. And speaking of time, we're running out of it. Let's get out of—"

The side exit door swung open, and Sean tucked in front of Sara. If anyone was going to take the fall for their nosing around in here, it would be him.

"Jimmy?" His former sergeant's name came off his tongue in an exhale of relief. Sean really didn't want to go to jail.

Sara stepped out from around Sean.

"Thought we met," Jimmy said.

"Very funny," Sean said. "What are you doing?"

"I just got finished taking this boy for a walkabout."

"Which we know," Sara interjected. "But how did you get in? Wasn't the door locked?"

Jimmy shook his head. "Nope. And I'll tell you something else. The guard is missing from this post."

"He was there earlier," Sean said. He'd even talked with him when he'd taken Magnum out.

"Well, he's gone now."

"What the…" Sean rubbed his head, thinking where the man could have gone and why.

"In one breath, the guys on the front door said there were no last-minute substitutions, yet in the next, the one who was to be posted at the side door went from being— One minute. I noted the names in my phone." Jimmy took out his phone and said, "Zeke Hale to Joe Mercer."

"Sounds like a substitution to me. You probably never pulled a background on Joe Mercer," Sean said.

"Nope."

The security company should have notified Jimmy immediately about any switch in staff. Their negligence might well be why Darlene Day was now dead. And Sean had met that man too. Thinking back on their interaction, he had seemed shifty.

"The guards don't even know each other, if you would believe it. They just get their marching orders and get to work." Jimmy tugged back gently on Magnum's leash, and the beagle sat. "Another thing you should know is the men at the front said Darlene Day told them to let Ralph Patrick in."

"Darlene?" Sara gasped. "Not possible. She didn't even like the man."

"Exactly as I thought."

"Seems like the killer falsely identified themselves as Darlene Day to make sure that Ralph Patrick was admitted." Sean did not like where any of this was going. So many holes...

Jimmy pressed his lips and nodded. "I think that's what happened."

"Our killer is a woman." Sara narrowed her eyes, her gaze disclosing she was deep in thought. "I just don't know how all the pieces fit together yet. Falsely impersonating Darlene, the fake invite, the two serving knives, the lapse in security, the unlocked door, and now the missing guard..."

"I can tell you what they add up to," Sean said. "Premeditated murder."

Chapter Twenty-One

A woman as the killer made sense, but it quickly eliminated Ralph Patrick from suspicion. But then, Sara recalled something they'd briefly touched on before. "What if we are looking at a partnership?"

Sean and Jimmy looked at each other, and they didn't need to say a word because she could sense they thought she'd lost her mind.

"Did you ask any of the guards about the missing one, once you noticed?" Sean asked Jimmy.

"Uh-huh, the guy on the back said he had to leave. Family emergency."

"Not so sure I'm buying it." Sean shook his head.

Sara understood his doubt. After all, the chances he was innocent were slim. "He's gone. Does that mean the woman who claimed to be Darlene Day is too?"

"I don't see how we could ever know for certain," Sean reasoned.

They needed more information on this Joe Mercer. If only they were free to leave, but Ryan insisted that the place be locked down. With that thought and realizing the breach left by the security company they hired, it would seem there wasn't much police presence outside. Otherwise, how had Jimmy walked around freely out there? And if he could do that, why couldn't he just slip away? "Were there police officers posted outside?"

"There are a couple out front."

"Would it be possible for you to sneak off and pull those backgrounds we need?" Sara asked.

"Maybe."

"Excellent. Go. And get back as fast as you can," she said.

"If you do this, Jimmy, you'll want to return before Doyle notices you're missing," Sean cautioned.

"Yeah, say that again. But you promise to have my back?"

"Always," Sara and Sean said in unison.

"All right, I'll give it a try. Message me the names you want backgrounds on."

"I can tell you some right now. Obviously, this Joe Mercer fella. Remember Austin Palmer? Add Ralph Patrick and…" She clamped her mouth shut, hating the thought of adding the names she was contemplating. "Molly Luna and Gertie Smith of Cotton Spring Falls."

Jimmy looked up from pecking into his phone. "And who are they?"

"Other potential suspects." She avoided looking at Sean even though she could feel him watching her.

Magnum bopped up and tugged at his leash again, and instead of reining him back, Jimmy handed it over to Sara.

"Wish me luck," he said before ducking back out the side door. "Text if any other names come up."

"We will," Sean responded, beating Sara to doing so.

Magnum whined when Jimmy left, and Sara hurried to her hunches to quiet him. She and Sean had been in here for long enough already, surely. And the last thing she needed was for the beagle to cause a fuss.

"We should leave," Sean said.

"Was thinking the same." She turned toward the door, but Magnum had a different idea.

He yanked the leash toward another door off the kitchen and pushed his nose against it.

The door opened to a coat closet, which must have been for staff, as it wasn't the main one. Sara hadn't even realized this room was here.

Magnum sniffed around and stopped, prying his nose into a lower shelf.

"What is it, buddy?" Sara moved quickly to prevent the beagle from barking because she had a feeling that was about to come. "It's a purse," she said, pulling out Magnum's find.

"Well, he likes something about it."

Sara opened the bag, despite her mind screaming to leave it alone. But what option did she and Sean have? If they brought it to Ryan, he'd cuff them for interfering. Inside there were keys, a makeup compact, a hairbrush, some tissue, a tube of a cheap-brand lipstick… Sara took the cap off. "Light pink…" She turned it over to read the label. "Coral blush." She recapped it and put it back. "No wallet, but—" She reached into an interior pocket and came out with a handful of feathers in different sizes from different birds. "Huh."

"Yeah, that can't be a coincidence." Sean raised his brows. "First, the dove feather under the island, and now this? It either means something to the case or Magnum doesn't like birds."

"Well, he is a hound, originally bred to accompany hunters. The dog's role is to retrieve what they shoot, often wild pheasant. But I don't think his bloodline is why Magnum's interested." Sara suspected it wasn't just about the feathers but rather some underlying scent that he picked up on. And if so, that would indicate the dove feather came from this purse. By extension, the killer may have removed something from the purse to which the feather had stuck. Then it just happened to fall under the counter during the murder.

"Sara, there's something else we need to consider. Look." Sean had moved to the other side of the room and was pushing on a door. She peeked through.

"I'll be."

"It leads to the second kitchen."

The implication of this discovery had another dose of adrenaline firing through her system. "This could be how the killer got away after stabbing Darlene—and why they weren't seen."

"Uh-huh, they slipped through the coatroom, out this door, and Bob's your uncle."

"Unbelievable." Ryan and his partner stepped into the doorway of the closet.

Talk about being caught red-handed.

"What are you two doing in here? And what is that?" Ryan jabbed a pointed finger at the purse in Sara's hand, as his gaze trailed more specifically to her palm that was full of feathers.

"Nothing." Sara tried to push the feathers back into the pocket of the purse, but some of them were stubbornly clinging to her fingers.

"I'll take that." Ryan snatched the bag from her, his hands gloved. "Where did you get this, and who does it belong to?"

"Got it from there." Sara indicated the spot Magnum had found it. "No idea who it belongs to." In her head, she was screaming, *the killer*, but had the brains not to say so out loud.

Ryan tucked the purse under one of his arms. "What are you doing in here? We've been through this. This kitchen is off-limits."

"Technically, we're not in the kitchen." Sara winced, and Ryan narrowed his eyes, not impressed. She started rambling despite herself. "We… we, ah." She was searching her mind for some excuse that might give them a stay-out-of-jail pass but came up empty.

Ryan snapped his fingers toward Louise, and in response she quirked an eyebrow as if to say she wasn't some dog he could boss around. "Cuff her. I'll get him. We'll have to figure out what to do with the dog."

"No. Please, Ryan," Sara pleaded. "You're making a mistake."

"I warned you, Sara." As Ryan snapped cuffs onto Sean's wrists, he solidified eye contact with Sara.

Boy, did I make a mistake inviting him to this party!

Chapter Twenty-Two

Jimmy stepped through the doors at the Albany Police station and took a deep breath. Leaving the venue had him feeling like a convict on the run. He kept looking in his rearview and side mirrors on the drive here, imagining that a CSFPD cruiser with flashing lights was going to pull up behind him. Thankfully, that fear turned out to be all in his head.

Now, to get done quickly what he was here to do and return before anyone clued into his absence.

He let himself into his office, opened the drawer in his desk, and withdrew a folder. It was where he had placed the backgrounds that he'd pulled on the assigned security guards. He looked for Joe Mercer, and as he'd suspected, he hadn't been part of the original crew.

Jimmy eased into his chair, and it groaned and squeaked beneath him in protest anyhow. He was past due for a new one, but restrictions on the department's budget didn't allow him the luxury of an upgrade. Flicking on his monitor, he logged on to the system and pulled Joe Mercer's background.

Resident of Albany, single, thirty-nine, no criminal record. Place of employment was listed as a pharmacy in the east end. That was curious, but it was entirely possible that the system was out of date.

Jimmy scrolled past known relations and stopped cold. One name screamed out from among the rest. Joe Mercer's cousin was Giles Cochran.

That was one person he'd never forget, even though it went back over fourteen years ago. A great mystery that he could remember that but not last week or what lunch was yesterday without giving it some thought. But the call had been one of Sean's first as a rookie cop, and Jimmy had been his training officer at the time. Sean had followed his intuition. It was a risky move that could have gotten people killed, but it hadn't. It might have even saved Cochran's life that day.

Cochran had held a convenience store clerk at gunpoint—passing off a water gun as the genuine article. He was arrested for attempted *armed* robbery, a charge Sean had fought hard to reduce to attempted robbery. But his efforts had been futile. The man also faced a charge of assault as he'd struck one customer—Douglas Quinn. The same man, as it turned out, from whom Sean ended up inheriting all his money.

Cochran would have been doled out a long prison sentence, but his case didn't get as far as trial. He'd killed himself in jail before then. He'd left a note saying that he wouldn't survive prison, and he apologized for his crimes.

As it turned out, not justification for his wrongdoings, but Cochran was in a desperate situation. He had lost everything in his life: his job, when the company he worked for fired him without just cause; his wife asked for a divorce; and his parents died in a car crash. All of that took place in the span of ten days. Cochran had snapped and wanted cigarettes but didn't have a penny to his name.

Before his life took those twists, Cochran had led a rather ordinary and peaceful existence.

And that was what Sean had seen—the desperation in him, not the desire to inflict harm. A man who was broken.

Jimmy sat back as he assimilated what this latest finding might mean. Did Joe Mercer hold Sean responsible for his cousin taking his own life? Was he out for revenge— possibly against Sean? He certainly had no business being a security guard at the wedding venue. His record had him employed at a pharmacy.

And if he was seeking vengeance, why come for it now, after all these years?

This didn't provide an answer as to where Mercer had gone, though. Why leave the venue? Had he gotten spooked and changed his mind? Or was he somewhere else on the premises planning to cause trouble? Was he at all involved with Darlene's murder?

Should Jimmy call Sean right now? But maybe he was making too much out of Mercer being at the venue. As he'd thought a moment ago, his place of employment on record may be out of date. There was one thing that could help him decide whether he was being overly cautious.

The other backgrounds would need to wait. He scribbled down the address for Zeke Hale—the guard scheduled to cover the side door—and ran out of his office. As he walked to his car, he reconsidered giving Sean a heads-up. After all, wasn't an ounce of prevention worth a pound of cure? Not to mention, if Mercer stepped in as a security guard, that presumably meant he was armed—wherever he was.

He texted Sean about Mercer and added that he and Sara may be in danger. Next, he called in to the station and had a Be-on-the-Lookout issued for Mercer's car.

He drove across the city, gas pedal to the floor, and pulled in front of Hale's house. Now here, it hit him that it might have been wise for him to dig deeper and see if there was any connection he could find between Mercer and Hale. It was possible they had coordinated the switch.

There was a muted light coming through blinds in a front window of Hale's home, but the exterior lights were off. There was a vehicle in the driveway.

Jimmy rang the doorbell and waited for a response for a few beats. Nothing.

He pushed the button a few more times, and it still didn't get him anywhere. He tried Hale's number and could hear a ringing phone coming from inside. Oh, he didn't have a good feeling about this.

He inched along the front of the house and rounded the corner. He found a window with the curtains open.

Jimmy stood up taller and peered inside. A man's limp form was seated on the couch, the TV on across from him.

I hate it when I'm right!

Jimmy made another call and waited for backup to arrive.

Chapter Twenty-Three

This was the night that would never end. In fact, with every passing second, somehow it felt like another hour got tagged on, and Sean was quite certain time was about to stretch even more. But surely Doyle would see reason and let them go.

Doyle and his partner had him, Sara, and Magnum segregated in one of the building's meeting rooms. At least they weren't being hauled away in cuffs. They still had them adorning their wrists, though.

Sean held up his arms. "Is this really necessary?"

"You tell me. When you were with the Albany PD and citizens interfered with a murder investigation, how did you handle it?" Doyle paced around in front of Sean and Sara, who were seated at the table.

Magnum was sitting between him and Sara at their feet, no one currently manning his leash.

Sean took a few moments to squash down his temper before responding. "I'd consider all the factors involved."

"You would? Really? Somehow, I don't believe that. And tell me, where's the older man?" Doyle looked at Louise Farmer for the name as if his memory had failed him.

"Sergeant Voigt," she said.

Doyle briefly held eye contact with his colleague. "For our purposes tonight, it's just Voigt. So, where is he? Last I saw him, he had the dog." Doyle danced his gaze between them.

"Did you check the restroom?" Sara asked.

Sean fought a grin from giving himself away. Sara never ceased to impress him. She could have lied, claimed they had no idea, but she hadn't. She'd deflected, presented a possibility instead of violating her ethics.

"We could, but I have the feeling he's not in the building." Doyle took a few steps, pivoted back.

Sean's phone chimed, and he cringed. He should have set it to silent after Jimmy left, but it wasn't like he had much chance. Magnum had been off following his nose, and he and Sara went after him, then… Well, they wound up here.

"Get his phone," Doyle told his partner.

Farmer rolled her eyes but did as she'd been told.

"You ever tire of him bossing you around?" Sean asked her as he directed her to his pocket.

"Part of the job," Farmer mumbled. She retrieved Sean's phone and held it up as if it were a trophy.

"Give it here."

"*Please* give it here," Sean said. "Use your manners."

Doyle glared at Sean. "You sit there in cuffs and feel you're in a position to antagonize me. You eager to go to jail?"

"Sean, please…" This came from Sara, and he looked over at her and nodded.

He'd cool it, even if it took mustering all his self-control to achieve that. And where had Hugh Thornton been all night anyhow? It was like their chosen master of ceremonies had sicced his detectives on them while he remained in the shadows.

"I didn't hear you, Mr. McKinley," Doyle said.

"No, I don't want to go to jail." He fought an eye roll. *Who wants to go to jail?* Doyle was obviously on a power trip.

"All right, then. Code or pattern to unlock your phone, *please*." Doyle held out a hand toward Farmer, and she dropped Sean's phone into his palm.

Sean told him the pattern to unlock the screen.

"Here we go. Let's see what we have." Doyle bit his bottom lip as he appeared to be reading. "Huh, it's a text from your friend Jimmy."

It took all of Sean's willpower not to push out the correction, *Sergeant Voigt* and add *show some respect*.

"He says that some guy named Joe Mercer is the missing guard, cousin of Giles Cochran, and that you and Sara may be in danger." Ryan looked up from the phone to Sara, then to Sean. "Who are these people?"

Just at the mention of Cochran's name, Sean's chest squeezed, and the past came hurtling back. "Long story."

"Best you start, then," Doyle said, adjusting his stance, putting one leg in front of the other as if he were settling in to stand for hours.

Sean took a deep breath. "I don't know who the Mercer fellow is—or didn't before this text—but Giles Cochran is someone I arrested." He could feel Sara's gaze on his profile and looked over at her. She angled her head, her eyes holding concern. She knew the story. "He killed himself while awaiting trial. He was in custody."

Farmer stepped in front of Sean, passed a side-glance at Doyle. "And this Mercer guy, that man's cousin, was here tonight?"

"Seems so. I mean, I know as much as you do about that," Sean admitted.

"What would any of this have to do with Day's murder this evening?" Farmer tapped her pen against her opened notebook.

"That I don't know," Sean said.

"And what does he mean *missing guard?*" Doyle asked.

Sean ran through that a team of four was to be posted and distributed to the three doors, then added, "There's only three around right now. You can check that for yourself. The one from the side door off the kitchen, where Darlene was murdered, isn't there." He withheld mention of Zeke Hale, who had been scheduled to work security.

"All right. And I'll ask one more time, where is Jimmy?" Doyle said.

"Where do you think, Ryan?" Sara pushed out. Her fury had Sean facing her, and he shook his head, hoping it would caution her not to provoke Doyle. Their roles were obviously in a state of reversal.

"What do—" Doyle snapped his mouth shut. It was like he was prepared with some pithy comeback, but Sara's response had caught him by surprise. Sean could understand why, as the attitude she'd shown was uncharacteristic for her.

"Ryan," Sara picked up, "Sergeant Voigt is checking on some things. We're sure that you and Detective Farmer have spoken to some people here who have raised some flags for you?"

Doyle and Farmer both nodded.

"And I don't see why we have to be coming at this like we're on opposing teams," Sara said.

"We have one of these." Doyle tapped the gold shield clipped to his waistband. "You don't. You're both civilians."

"Could you get over yourself?" Sara blurted out.

The room fell silent for several seconds. *Stunned* silence.

Sara was the one to bring it to an end. "Sean and I have several years between us working in Homicide. We have a lot vested in the discovery of Darlene Day's killer. You know me, Ryan. I grew up knowing Darlene, eating her freshly baked cookies and cakes—some for my birthday parties that you were invited to." Now the edge was gone from her voice, and she resembled the woman Sean knew.

Sean briefly met Farmer's gaze, and hers softened. It was hard to say what was going through Doyle's mind.

A few seconds passed in silence before Sara broke it. "Can't we just work together on this?"

"Ry, she might have a point here," Farmer said. "Two heads are better than one, and in this case four instead of two. Yeah?"

Doyle huffed out a breath. "Fine. We'll uncuff them."

Sean clamped his mouth shut so as not to say something smart-alecky while Doyle undid the ones on his wrists. Farmer got the pair off Sara.

"We might do well to start off by finding out who owns that purse we found," Sara said.

Sean hated to disagree with his bride-to-be, but… "I think we should start with Jimmy's text. Take it seriously. He said we could be in danger, and this Mercer guy is missing. He might have hightailed it from here, but he could be around. Without knowing what he might have planned, we best not take any risks. We need to locate him."

Doyle held up a hand. "Let's take a few deep breaths before we get all carried away."

The admonition had Sean's temper sparking. He wasn't one to easily get riled up and didn't appreciate being viewed as such a person. But he managed to keep quiet—for Sara's sake. But if Mercer was acting as a guard, that meant he was likely carrying a gun too. None of this was boding well… "Just thought of something," Sean rushed out quickly.

"What?" Doyle said, impatient and exasperated.

"We could try raising Mercer on the radio. Surely, he'd have one if he was playing guard. He probably won't answer, but we need to try."

Doyle motioned for Farmer to do just that, and she wasn't gone long.

Farmer returned, shaking her head. "No answer, as you suspected."

Sean felt it had been worth a try.

"Now that's out of the way," Doyle said, "tell us what you've learned."

Sean didn't feel *that* was out of the way at all. Mercer was out there—he could feel it. As for sharing what he and Sara had learned, he had the urge to withhold his hand like he would in a poker game, but now wasn't the time for such a strategy—not if he wanted to stay out of jail. "You see the purse." He gestured toward where it was currently on the table. "We just found it where we showed you—"

"Okay," Doyle dragged out. "What's so special about it?"

You might know already if you didn't interrupt me!

"What's so *special* about it, Ryan, is it may belong to the killer," Sara said.

Sean glanced over at her. It felt like she was putting a lot of faith in that being the case. Though he could see the location where the sole feather was found—near where Darlene had been stabbed—being curious. And it would be easier to dismiss if it wasn't for a purse housing a collection of feathers. Despite that, was it the killer's bag or coincidental? He wasn't sure.

"You disagree?" Farmer said, as she must have picked up on some tell in Sean's facial expression.

"I'm not saying that," Sean said.

Sara picked up and told them about the feather under the counter. "You did collect the feather from under the cabinet?"

Doyle looked at Farmer. "Did you hear if the CSIs collected any?"

Farmer rolled her eyes. "I told you they did."

"I must have just dismissed it."

"You can't dismiss anything in a murder case, Ryan," Sara said. "And now we have this purse, and there are a lot more feathers in it." She pointed to it on the table. "Go ahead and look for yourself. Interior pocket."

"I saw them in your hand when we caught you snooping around, remember?" Doyle said. "But how can you know that a single feather found on the floor and this purse are tied to the killer?"

"Ryan," Sara began. "It's too odd not to be. You heard me when I told you that the single feather was found right where Darlene was stabbed?"

Doyle massaged his left temple, and Sean understood how he felt. Trying to unravel everything that transpired tonight felt like trying to align one giant Rubik's Cube—and he'd never understood them to begin with.

"We don't have all the answers yet ourselves," Sean eventually said after the silence had stretched out for a bit. His phone pinged again, still in Doyle's hand. "If I could…" Sean held out an open palm toward the detective.

Doyle seemed to hesitate but gave it to him.

Sean looked at the new message, and his entire body stiffened. "It's from Jimmy. The guard who was scheduled to work tonight may be dead."

Sara put her hand on Sean's forearm, her eyes widening slightly. "We should take Jimmy's warning seriously about this Mercer fellow."

"So it would seem," Sean agreed.

"Hold up here. There was another guard scheduled to work, but this Joe Mercer turned up instead?"

"Yep. Now you're all caught up," Sean said.

"Name?" Farmer asked.

"Zeke Hale."

"And now you're telling me this Hale guy didn't show because he's dead?" Doyle raised his brows and angled his head.

Doyle can't be accused of being a fast study… "I realize it's a lot to keep up with, but yes, that's exactly what Jimmy's telling us."

"You need to send him a message and get him back here ASAP." Doyle drove a pointed finger toward the floor.

"Ryan." It was Sara again, her voice soft and submissive. "We all know Jimmy didn't kill Darlene. Let him carry on doing what he's doing out there. You have us here, and between the four of us, if there's something to find here, we will."

Ryan huffed out a breath and clenched his jaw. His gaze took a brief trip somewhere else, then he pushed out, "Fine."

"That means we can ask our guests questions and have free rein to look around?" Sara asked.

"Within reason. What do you have in mind?"

"First off, did you find Darlene's purse and phone?" Sara asked.

Sean thought Sara might lay out all their suspicions to this guy, but it was best they get what they could from him and Farmer, not the other way around.

"We have it, yes," Farmer said.

Sara went on. "Did it point at anyone who had an issue with Darlene?"

Doyle narrowed his eyes and ignored Sara's question. "How do we know that Darlene wasn't just an innocent casualty? She could have stumbled across Mercer's plans, whatever they were, and out of fear of being exposed, he stabbed her and ran off."

Sara opened her arms and gestured that it was possible. "Very well could be the case."

Sean could give Doyle's theory merit if not for a few things—the fake invite and letter to Ralph Patrick, the second serving knife, and the fact Sean talked to Mercer after the murder. His *running off* didn't come until some later point—that was, if he had. If his cop instincts were right, two things had been at play tonight. While Darlene had been a victim, only time would tell his and Sara's fate. But if Sean had a say, they'd come out of this alive and unharmed.

"We need to get cars around to Mercer's house and see if he's at home," Doyle said.

"I'm sure Jimmy will have that checked out, but if Mercer came here with a plan—and I doubt it was to kill Darlene—that means he's still around here somewhere," Sean said.

Doyle set his lips in a straight line. "Very well. But Jimmy needs to talk to me and keep me in the loop too."

"You got it. I'll text him right now. Your number?" Sean asked.

Doyle gave it to him, and Sean messaged Jimmy that the Cotton Spring Falls PD was working with them and to keep Doyle up to date. "Text sent—" A quick chime back, and Sean had Jimmy's response.

Tell Mr. Doyle, Mercer and Hale are in Albany jurisdiction.

"What did he say?" Ryan asked.

"That he'd be happy to cooperate." Sean pressed on a smile, justifying his answer, as Jimmy hadn't refused.

"Good. All right, Louise, let's get back to work."

"And us?" Sara asked.

"Find a way to entertain yourselves, but don't get in our way." Doyle turned and left the room with Farmer following close behind.

Sara angled toward Sean. "I'd say we've made some headway with him."

"Seems so. At least we have some freedom of movement."

"Let's go do something with it."

He hesitated.

"What is it, Sean?"

"We need to be careful. We're left with the fact that someone here wants to get revenge on us, and he very well may still be around."

"I know. It's possible Darlene found out about what Mercer had planned and silenced her too. It might explain why Darlene came to the bridal suite. To warn us? But how does icing make any sense?"

"We could also be looking at two entirely different things. Mercer was here for us, and Darlene's killer came for her. Remember, it was a woman who told the front security guys to let Ralph Patrick in. Where do you say we start?"

"With Molly and Gertie while watching our backs."

"Let's do it, then." Sean was the first to stand and gestured for Sara to get up. He hugged her and kissed her brow line, sweeping a hand over her hair. "I love you."

"I love you." Sara got to her haunches and rubbed Magnum's head. "And we both love you."

Sean smiled despite the danger they might be in. She was the sweetest, most gentle soul he knew, and he would do all that was necessary to protect the woman he loved. He also had high ambitions to find justice for Darlene Day in the process.

Chapter Twenty-Four

Jimmy was regretting letting Sara and Sean rope him into all this, and now that kid detective expected Jimmy to answer to him. Dream on. To start, he had no real cause to continue holding him—or anyone, for that matter—at the venue. Then there was the matter of Hale's residency falling into Jimmy's jurisdiction. Same applied to Joe Mercer. Uniformed officers should be on their way there now to see if, by chance, he turned up.

Jimmy let himself through Hale's front door and stormed right into the living room. After seeing his motionless form, it gave him enough cause. "Albany PD! Zeke Hale? Do you hear me?"

The cool feeling in the room was cloying, like when there was a death. This sensation intensified when it was due to murder.

Jimmy moved closer to Hale. Still no reaction to his call—verbal or otherwise. He repeated himself, and this netted a response. Hale groaned, stirred, then panicked. A wide-eyed Hale shuffled to sit up straight.

"Whoa, whoa! Hold up, man! Who are you? Why are you in my home?" Hale's eyes were bloodshot, and he was holding up his hands in surrender, more fearful than capable of defending himself. "Please get out!"

He even has manners… "Albany PD. Sergeant Voigt."

"Congratulations, but what are you doing in my house? And you're a cop?" Hale seemed to be waking more from his stupor with every passing second.

"A sergeant, but that's not—"

"A little overdressed, ain't ya?"

Jimmy had been so focused on his mission that he'd forgotten he was still dressed in a tux. How he'd managed not to run into anyone at the station was a shocker too. If he had, they'd have pointed out his attire. "Long story. Listen, are you okay? I saw you through your front window, and I thought that…" Jimmy stumbled over the right words in his head. Somehow, telling the living, breathing man he thought he was dead didn't feel right. It also wouldn't exactly build the man's confidence in his policing skills. But in Jimmy's defense, he had appeared unconscious.

"I don't know." Hale was slurring, and he rubbed the back of his head. "I feel like I've been hit by a freight train."

Jimmy looked around, and there weren't any empty alcohol bottles or evidence that he'd smoked weed or taken any other type of narcotic. There was a bottle of prescription pills on the table next to him. Jimmy picked it up and read the label. Amoxicillin.

It was often prescribed for infections and couldn't have caused Hale to pass out.

The pharmacy logo had the back of Jimmy's neck tightening, though. It was where Mercer worked. Could he have tampered with them—his plan to take Hale's place at the venue?

"Did you take these?" Jimmy held up the bottle and shook it, the pills that remained inside clicking against each other.

Hale's forehead was scrunched like he had a headache. "Ah, yeah, I have a bit of an ear infection."

"When did you take them?"

"Just— Oh, no, what time is it?" Hale looked out through the open window. "It's nighttime. Shoot, I have somewhere I need to be."

"Just slow down there, tiger. I think someone drugged you." That was how Jimmy framed it, but there was no *think* about it. Rather, it felt like a guarantee. Mercer, wherever he was, was up to no good.

"Who would want to do that?"

"How many did you take?"

"Two, maybe three. I can't remember now."

Jimmy snapped the cap off and dumped a few tablets into his palm. These weren't amoxicillin. He recognized the color and stamp pushed into them. They were a rather strong over-the-counter sleep medication. The recommended dose was one, and Hale had taken two to three times that amount. No wonder he had been Sleeping Beauty. "Where did you get these?"

"The pharmacy name is on the label, isn't it? I always go there for my prescriptions."

"On a regular schedule?"

"Usually at this point in the month, yeah. I have asthma and acid reflux and the prescriptions keep them under control."

"Anyone different serve you or prepare it?"

"I dunno. Listen, I really need to get going. I'm probably beyond late." Hale moved awkwardly as if trying to stir his limbs into cooperating.

"You're going to stay put while I call for paramedics to come take a quick look at you."

"That's really unnecessary."

"You took two, maybe three sleeping pills. The regular recommended dose is one. Might be a good idea. And I probably don't need to point out that you were down for the count."

"I don't understand why anyone would— Oh. *Ooooohhhh.* The tux. Are you here from the wedding? Is everything okay? I had every intention of getting there. I swear. Even with the ear infection."

"I imagine you did. But don't you worry about any of that. Just sit there while I make some calls." Jimmy didn't see a point in adding to his mental burden by telling him there had been a murder. They didn't even know if or how Mercer tied into it, but it seemed clear Hale wasn't involved.

"Okay."

Jimmy stepped out of the living room and called paramedics to come look at Hale. By the time he hung up with them, his phone was ringing.

He answered and listened to the officer that was at Mercer's house. The message wasn't one he wanted to hear, but not a surprise all the same.

No one was home.

Jimmy didn't like any of this one bit. Where was Joe Mercer, and what did he have planned? Regardless, one thing was apparent: it was time to take the threat of Joe Mercer's presence at the venue seriously. They couldn't assume he'd left the community center.

He pulled out his phone, hands shaking as he selected Sean's contact and made the call.

Chapter Twenty-Five

Sara expected to die one day. It was a fact of life. And once she'd donned the badge, she half expected she might meet her end in a standoff with a criminal. But when she and Sean left their life with the PD behind, she had assumed any real threat to their well-being ended there too. She was wrong. And she should have known better. She'd seen firsthand how people returned for revenge due to a past perceived wrongdoing. Sometimes years after the fact. Revenge didn't seem to have a statute of limitations. Rather, the feeling of rage sat dormant until it was triggered. So what had recently triggered Joe Mercer?

Jimmy had said she *and* Sean were in danger, but it would make sense that Joe Mercer's primary target would be Sean. Then again, she shouldn't rush to assume that. Mercer may intend to use Sara as leverage to lure Sean out or hurt him in return. Eye-for-an-eye mentality. Kill a loved one of Sean's, as he viewed Sean to blame for his cousin's suicide.

Sean's phone rang. He touched her arm, and they both stepped to the side of the hallway. "It's Jimmy," he said before answering on speaker.

"Hale's alive, but his prescription was substituted for sleeping pills," Jimmy said. "It's a long story, but all you should concern yourself with is that Joe Mercer's location is unknown. He's not at home. He could be anywhere, but I think it's best to assume he's there, likely inside the venue. Right now."

As if Jimmy needed to add *right now*. Trembles ran through Sara's body.

"I had an interaction with this guy earlier," Sean said, and it had Sara turning to face him, her mouth agape. "Nothing happened, but he was shifty. Just fire me over his picture, Jimmy, and we'll look out for him."

"And share this with Ryan and Louise." She and Sean couldn't play aloof with the detectives anymore. The threat was alive and well, and it was best they get all the help they could on this one.

"Doing that next. Just please, please, *please* watch your backs."

"We will," Sean said. "And you too."

"You got it. No one dies today." It was a mantra that Jimmy used all the time.

"Amen to that," Sean replied, and Jimmy was gone.

"Mercer could still be here." *Around the next corner…* When it was a possibility he had left, there was still hope. That was now gone.

"It's possible, yes. But just because he isn't home, it doesn't mean he's here. Even Jimmy said he could be anywhere." Sean was level-headed at the most stressful of times. It was a characteristic of his she had come to rely on.

"I think we both know that's not true. He's here."

"He could have gotten spooked and changed his plan to come after us because of Darlene's murder."

Sara shook her head. "I appreciate what you're trying to do, Sean, but I don't need you to shelter me. This Mercer guy is intent. He drugged that security guard to take his place. He planned ahead. I don't see him just giving up and going away."

Sean didn't say anything for a few beats, then, "At least he didn't kill him. He also didn't hurt me, and he could have. We were outside alone. I mean we could take some comfort in both those things, right? Maybe he's not a cold-blooded killer."

"The timing could have been wrong, and he probably doesn't have any issue with Hale. Drugging him could have just been a means to an end." She paused there, not about to lay it out in black and white—that they were that *end*. "We can't afford the luxury of deceiving ourselves into thinking we're safe."

Sean's phone chimed, and he held up the screen for them both to see.

Joe Mercer looked like an average Joe—brown hair, brown eyes—with a small scar line across his forehead and thin lips. He certainly didn't look like an evil man, but Sara had learned from years on the police force, sometimes the most genteel looking of people housed the most maniacal minds.

"Let's just check in with Doyle and Farmer and make sure Jimmy sent this to them too," Sean said. "I wouldn't put it past Jimmy to keep them out of the loop."

She nodded, imagining that was possible but questioning if Jimmy would take such a stand considering the risk.

Sara scanned the crowd, looking for the face she'd just committed to memory and didn't see him anywhere. That didn't mean he wasn't out there lurking in the shadows.

She did spot Ryan and Louise—he was with Sean's aunt Gwen, and Louise was chatting with Sara's parents. Molly and Gertie, who she and Sean had intended to speak with, were talking in a corner.

"You coming with me?" Sean brushed his hand against her arm.

She gestured toward Molly and Gertie. "I'm going to carry on with what we were going to do."

"All right. I'll catch up with you in a minute."

Sean walked off toward Ryan while she and Magnum headed in the opposite direction.

Molly and Gertie both pouted as Sara approached, and both insisted on hugging her.

"Oh, dearie, I'm so sorry." Molly rubbed her back during their embrace.

Gertie tapped a kiss to each of Sara's cheeks. Both women cooed over Magnum for a few seconds.

"Thank you, ladies. But who I feel bad for is Trinity." Sara wasn't sure why that had slipped from her mouth. She had meant to say Darlene, and while she'd been the one to lose her life, she was beyond the reach of pain. Trinity, assuming she was innocent as Sara suspected, would be dealing with grief for a long time.

"Oh, that girl will be just fine." Molly rolled her eyes and tapped Gertie's arm.

"Uh-huh," Gertie agreed.

Sara stiffened. "I don't understand. Darlene was her aunt. She took her in when her parents died, loved her as if she were her own child. You make it sound like she'll just bounce right back."

"Except she wasn't, now, was she?" Molly pushed back.

"What are you saying?"

Darlene hadn't supported Trinity's dream of becoming a ballet dancer, but these women were making it sound as if there was something deeper amiss in the aunt/niece relationship.

Gertie looked at Molly, back to Sara. "From the very begin—" Gertie softly winced as if she were in pain or uncomfortable and laid a hand on her stomach. She then added, "Those two are as different as oil and water. And I ought to know."

"She's right, Sara," Molly chimed in. "Gertie lives next door."

"Yep, and I have heard plenty of fights between the two over the last couple of years."

"About what?"

"Unfortunately, I couldn't get it all. Their voices didn't come through that clearly. In fact, it wasn't until…" Gertie stopped talking as Sean stepped up beside Sara.

He captured the attention of both women. Sara made eye contact with him, and he subtly nodded. She sensed he had something to tell her, but it would have to wait. Gertie was just about to say something, and Sara wanted to find out what that was. "Sean, Molly and Gertie were just telling me that Darlene and her niece didn't always see eye to eye."

Molly and Gertie chuckled as if Sara's wording downplayed reality. Gertie's amusement was cut short as another wince contorted her expression.

"Are you all right?" Sara touched the woman's shoulder.

"Yeah, I'm fine." Another tremor tore through her, betraying her words, but she waved off Sara's concern with a sweep of her hand.

Sara had no choice but to take the older woman's word for it, and picked up the conversation where it had left off before Sean's arrival. "You said their voices were never clear until…?"

"*Until* yesterday."

If it had been Trinity at the restaurant, the argument may have resumed when they got home. The dynamics between aunt and niece were really messing with Sara's head. "What time was this?"

"In the afternoon, just as I was making dinner. Say around four thirty. I like to eat early, so I have time to digest." Gertie winced again and rubbed her stomach this time.

That would have been before Sara had overheard Darlene in the restaurant's kitchen. She would inquire about Gertie's health again but figured she'd just dismiss it as she had last time. She was still interested in what Gertie may have heard. "What were they saying?"

"It was probably the biggest fight they had."

Sara should have known Gertie would take her sweet time to get to the point. The woman was a natural at making a short story long. "What was it about?"

"Well, from what I could piece together, Trinity wanted to marry Austin."

Sara looked wide-eyed at Sean. That was certainly news, but did it affect Darlene's fate?

"I take it Darlene was against the union?" Sean said.

"You betcha. Trinity's just a kid with her entire life ahead of her. Dar tried to tell her that, but the niece was having none of it," Gertie said. "Dar even brought up the argument about Juilliard. Put it in her face, didn't she want to go, that it would be impossible to pursue a career in dance *and* maintain a marriage. It's a lot of work, you know." It would seem the latter bit was tacked on for her and Sean. And while Sara knew logically that maintaining a solid marriage would take effort and compromise, her relationship with Sean didn't feel like work.

"It definitely takes maturity," Sean said as he slipped his arm around Sara's waist, and she melted against his side. She took his sign of affection to mean that he felt the same way as she did. They just fit.

"Those kids ain't got that," Molly said.

"What was Trinity's response to Darlene pointing out how hard it would be to balance marriage and training for a career in ballet?" Sara asked.

"She told Dar she would do whatever she wanted, and there was nothing she could do to stop her. Of course, she used the opportunity to put out there she was an adult now."

"In age only," Molly put in. "Otherwise, her level of maturity leaves a lot to be desired."

She had known these two were chatty and sized up everyone they encountered, but she hadn't realized how nasty their talk could get, how judgmental. Had she just forgotten this aspect about them, choosing instead to look at their good qualities, or were they painting Trinity in a bad light to deflect any attention off them? That latter thought fired through. After all, the reason she and Sean wanted to talk to them originally was because they had opposed Darlene's take on advancement. Also, Gertie due to her love for feathers. Yet it wasn't coming across that they had any issue with Darlene personally. If anything, they did with Trinity.

Gertie pressed her lips together, and her eyes narrowed from an obvious jab of pain. She waved a hand at Sara and said, "I told you, I'm fine. It's just late, and I should have known better than to eat cake at this hour. Dang indigestion."

"I have an antacid if you'd like." Molly rooted in her purse and pulled out a small sleeve of them.

"You're a gem." Gertie took one, popped it into her mouth, and chomped away.

"I did warn you not to eat the cake." Molly primly tucked the antacids back into her bag, apparently not able to do so without rubbing in, *I told so.*

Cake… *Icing.* Sara couldn't shake this horrible feeling that washed over her. Hadn't Trinity said that Darlene was unwell and had cramps? And since then, she and Sean had concluded Darlene had eaten some cake. Could it be that the *icing* had made her sick, and Darlene figured this out and tried to warn Sara? Even if that was the case, how did it have any bearing on her murder? "Do you have cramps?" Sara could barely get the words out.

"Yes, but it's no big deal. I get them sometimes."

"Excuse us." Sara turned to Sean and pulled him away from the women. Magnum tagged along with them. Once out of earshot, she said to Sean, "Icing."

His face was blank.

"Sean, Darlene ate some cake, and Trinity told us she had cramps when she'd seen her. What if someone tampered with the icing, Darlene found out who had done it, and confronted them?" She had just needed a few seconds to conjure a theory of how icing may have led to murder.

"Mercer," Sean said, letting the name fall out on a long breath.

"Could be that was Mercer's plan all along. It was put into motion, and he left?"

"But he was around after Darlene's death, remember? Though, of course you do."

"So he left after that."

"Hate to say it, Sara, but if Mercer is out for revenge, he's going to want to witness what he's done."

"All right, well, he still could have poisoned the icing, but that would also mean he is around here still." Sara stopped talking and scanned the room. A lot of their guests were looking uncomfortable—their expressions tinged with pain. "We need to stop serving the cake immediately and get everyone medical attention!"

Chapter Twenty-Six

Sara tapped Sean's arm, urging him to yell to get everyone's attention. She doubted her voice would carry.

"Everyone, please stop eating the cake!" Sean shouted.

Only the people closest to them turned in their direction. His voice wasn't strong enough to carry through the entire room either.

"The microphone, Sean." She gestured toward the front of the room. It had been intended for speeches and announcements. She just never would have expected one like this.

Sean took off running in its direction while she made her way over to Vanessa, who was still doling out pieces of cake.

"Stop," Sara told the woman.

Vanessa set down the cake knife but licked a trace of icing from a fingertip.

"Oh, you shouldn't have done that." Sara took the plate from Sean's aunt, and the woman appeared startled and confused. "There's something wrong with it," she told her.

Gwen's eyes widened. "What do you mean there's something wrong with it?"

Sean's voice came over the speakers in the room. "Excuse me, everyone, I need your immediate attention."

Sara gestured toward a uniformed officer and asked that he stand next to the cake and ensure that no one eat it or touch it. Then she grabbed the garbage bin near the table and went to the people around her and had them toss whatever they had left.

Sean continued. "We have reason to believe that the cake may have been tampered with—"

A collective gasp. Then silence. The guests were looking at each other, at Sara, their eyes seeking an explanation. "Please, just throw it out." She collected all the plates and bits of leftover cake she could.

Ryan headed to Sean, while Louise was beelining for Sara.

"What is going on?" Louise asked her.

"Long story, but it's likely the icing or the cake itself was poisoned or drugged. We don't know with what or the extent of harm it may cause yet. We need to get paramedics on scene immediately to check everyone over."

Louise pulled out her cell phone and made the call, and Sara appreciated that the woman trusted what she'd said and didn't argue it to death or pull it apart. Then again, she wasn't Ryan.

Sean cupped the microphone, and he and Ryan put their heads together in conversation. Shortly after, Sean spoke to the crowd again. "Anyone who isn't feeling well or who ate any cake at all, go to the right of the room, and we'll have you looked over by a medic."

"Detective Farmer is calling it in now," Sara yelled as loud as she could manage. With the quieted room, it reached Sean's ears, which she knew because he gave her a thumbs up.

Ryan nudged Sean to the side and spoke into the mike. "It's important that no one panics. We have this under control."

Sara would have rolled her eyes if so many people weren't watching for her reaction. They had nothing under control—at all.

"But please, do as Mr. McKinley has just directed." Ryan gestured for people to line up on the right of the room.

Sara's shoulders sank as at least two thirds of their guests shuffled there, including Vanessa, who had just licked a finger of icing. So many of them didn't look well, their steps slowed. For everyone who passed her, a stab of guilt cut through her. It burrowed deeper when she saw Officer Simms clutching his abdomen. She'd brought cake to him. But all of these people were sick because she and Sean had an enemy. These people were innocent. Among the throng were her parents and her best friends, a few of her former colleagues, and Sean's friend Conrad.

Tears pricked Sara's eyes. *Please, please let them be okay!*

"Paramedics will be here soon," Louise informed Sara. "I also called in CSIs. They'll need to collect samples of the cake and see if they can determine what the contaminant might be."

"I don't think it's the cake itself, rather the icing," Sara told her. "Have them focus on that."

Louise nodded. "Because Day's last word to you was *icing?*"

"Uh-huh. I think she was trying to warn us that she discovered someone had messed with it."

"Do you think this someone is Mercer?" Louise asked.

"I don't know the guy, but he did drug the security guard who was supposed to work today. It could reflect a pattern for him." Sara had slipped right back into cop talk.

"Good point. Well, we have officers actively searching for him in and around the building. No dice yet. I assume Sean told you Mercer's car was found parked a few blocks over."

Sara's legs crumpled, and she shook her head. That must have been what Sean was going to tell her. "He's probably hanging around, then. Maybe even in this room."

Louise and Sara looked around. Sara concentrated on the third of the guests still on the left. None of them were Joe Mercer—unless he was disguised. There was also the possibility that he was passing himself off as someone who had eaten the cake, on the right. Either way, Sara had this niggling feeling he was close by.

Sean and Ryan joined Sara and Louise. It was nice to see them as a united front instead of butting horns.

"Wow, this night continues to get more and more exciting," Desiree Moore purred as she stepped up to the group of them. "I see an article on page one." She swiped her arm in an arc overhead as if indicating her name in lights.

"You shouldn't even be here," Sara pushed back.

"What do you mean, Sara?" Ryan asked and cocked his head. Sara knew that mannerism meant he was looking for one good reason to cuff Desiree. Far be it from Sara to deny him that pleasure.

"Ms. Moore here was never on the guest list."

One eyebrow curved up. "Oh really? It seems we need to have a little talk."

Desiree simpered at Sara and rolled her eyes. "Ms. Cain is making a big hullabaloo about nothing, Detective Doyle."

"I don't think she is," Ryan said. "This venue is the scene of a murder and possibly a mass poisoning. That means any anomalies need to be examined thoroughly. And if I need to spell it out, you, Ms. Moore, are an anomaly."

Sara was smiling while the smug expression disappeared from Desiree's face.

"How did you get in here?" Ryan asked her.

Desiree was quiet. *That's a first…*

"Ms. Moore," Ryan prompted.

"I came in through the side door."

"The guard there let you in?" Sean said, his voice firm.

"No one was there at the time."

Sara wondered how long Mercer had been gone from the side door. He was there after Darlene's murder, as Sean had spoken to him, but between then and them running into Desiree, he'd apparently taken off somewhere. It was the *where* part that was both a mystery and unsettling.

"That door opens right into the kitchen in which Ms. Day was murdered," Ryan deadpanned.

Desiree pulled back, offended. It was impressive she was still determined to hold her ground. "I certainly didn't kill her."

"It would give you that page-one article," Louise pointed out.

Sara was starting to really like the woman.

"I don't need to murder someone to make page one," Desiree seethed.

"It wouldn't hurt, though, would it?" Ryan said. "You weren't even invited to one of the biggest weddings this area has ever had."

Desiree glanced at Sara. "We ended up coming to an arrangement."

"Technically, no promises were made," Sara said stiffly.

"What time did you let yourself in?" Ryan asked.

Desiree prattled off a time that fit what Sara had concluded. From the sound of it, not long after Sean had spoken with Mercer.

"Was anyone in the kitchen at that time?" Sara asked.

"Nope."

Ryan's face bunched up, and it clicked for Sara why. Officer Simms should have been watching the kitchen during that time. "How did you get out of the kitchen?" she asked Desiree.

"Through the door."

Sara narrowed her eyes. "More specifically?"

"I ducked through the adjacent coatroom and exited through the other kitchen."

Sara and Ryan briefly made eye contact, and he subtly dipped his head. Her question had cleared Officer Simms of being negligent in his duties. It had also exposed a hole in cordoning off the crime scene. Were officers not posted at the other kitchen or the dining hall?

"Well, you've still got my interest." Ryan summoned for a nearby uniformed officer to take Desiree to the meeting room where he'd spoken with her and Sean.

"Since you're gathering people of interest, get your hands on Ralph Patrick too." While she and Sean had let him slip from suspicion, it didn't hurt to sequester the one other person who wasn't invited.

"Who is Ralph Patrick?" Louise asked.

They didn't discover him on their own? She tried to mask her shock. What had she and Ryan been doing for the last number of hours? "He's with the Bakery Box.

They wanted to acquire Darlene's shop, but she had zero interest in selling to them."

"I know about the Bakery Box," Ryan said. "How did the guy get in?"

"A fake invite that someone took a lot of trouble to produce, and there was a letter with it signed by Darlene, but it was a forgery," Sara said.

"Jeez, there seems to be a lot of moving parts to today's events," Louise said.

"Sean and I theorized that someone had planned to kill Darlene and arranged for Ralph Patrick's attendance so he could be a patsy," Sara explained. "But now with Mercer in the mix and the tainted icing… I'm not sure exactly what to think anymore. There's also the fact that some woman claiming to be Darlene okayed his admission with a guard at the front door."

Ryan raised his eyebrows, and his voice increased an octave. "A woman?"

"What we were told," Sean inserted.

"Huh. Thought we were looking at Joe Mercer." Ryan's jaw tightened in concentration.

"Sean and I think he might have been out for revenge on us—the tainted icing, possibly? Then Darlene found out, Mercer felt his plan was threatened, and took her out."

"Still doesn't explain this woman who wanted Patrick here," Ryan pushed out.

"It's possible having him here was part of a more elaborate plan." Sara shrugged. She didn't know what to think anymore, except there was a mystery woman and Mercer to consider.

"A partnership of sorts," Louise said, nodding. "Mercer and this woman."

Sara latched her gaze with Louise. "Could be. But the invite must have been copied by someone we invited. It had similar elements to its design, and they knew one was needed to get into the venue."

"That's where you might be wrong again, Sara," Ryan said.

"In what regard?"

"Darlene was so excited about your wedding that she posted your invite on the community board in Locally Baked for months. Patrick could have easily seen it there and concocted a plan to gain entrance today. He could have also forged that letter that was supposedly from Darlene."

"If that's the case, it wouldn't explain the woman claiming to be Darlene vouching for him," Sara reasoned.

Ryan held up his hands. "Just brainstorming out loud."

It could be that Ralph Patrick and this mystery woman weren't even involved with Darlene's murder. Maybe this woman had simply wanted to upset Darlene's day by bringing in the rep from the Bakery Box. But how did that explain the feather near the murder scene and more of the same in a woman's purse? Was any of that relevant? What was glaring now was the fact the icing had been tampered with—that was beyond doubt as she looked around at her and Sean's loved ones, taking in the pain on their faces. Mercer was likely behind this, and without knowing where he was, he remained a threat. And him being behind the poisoning lined up as she'd said to Louise. She voiced this opinion again to the group. "It makes sense Mercer could attack us by tampering with the icing. He did substitute Hale's prescription."

"Sleeping pills, not poison," Sean countered.

"We don't know there's poison in the icing. It could just be something to make people ill," she said.

"But why would Mercer show up after fifteen years—supposedly for revenge—and make his show that? He'd be out for blood," Sean said.

"I'm not going to dispute that, but as we discussed before, Sean, Mercer could have killed Hale. He didn't. There's also the possibility we're looking at two unrelated incidents—Darlene's murder and whatever has brought Mercer here." The possibilities were bouncing around in her head like ping-pong balls.

Ryan sighed loudly.

"Laced icing would also be an attack on Darlene's bakery," Louise said. "It could have been done to taint her reputation."

"If that is the case, it's likely not Mercer," Sara reasoned. "What are the chances he's from Sean's past and wanted Darlene out of business? He's not even from Cotton Spring Falls."

"All right, then we might do well to ask who would want to jeopardize the bakery. Who would benefit from destroying its reputation?" Sean put out there.

Several paramedics swept into the room and started seeing to those who were ill. Sara couldn't stay put any longer and excused herself to check on her family and best friends.

As she hurried across the room with Magnum, the dangling questions that were raised and the uncertainty of Mercer's plans haunted her.

Chapter Twenty-Seven

Sean left Ryan and Louise and trailed behind Sara and Magnum. He saw Conrad standing among those who had eaten cake, and his friend's face was knotted in anguish. He excused himself from Sara and joined his friend. "Talk to me, buddy."

"It's just some cramps, but they are powerful." Conrad's forehead was beaded with sweat.

"How much cake did you eat?" Sean didn't really need to ask. His friend had a hollow leg.

"You know me. I have a healthy appetite."

"An actual answer?"

"Three good-sized pieces, but don't judge. I was starving."

"No judgment at all, believe me." Sean gripped his friend's shoulder and did his best to cling to the wish that whatever was in the icing wasn't deadly. "Just give me a minute." Sean intercepted the closest medic, who was about to go to someone else, and motioned him to check Conrad next. "He ate a lot and isn't doing well," Sean told him.

The medic nodded and came over to Conrad, got his name as he started to do some tests. He took his blood pressure and listened to his heart, took his temperature.

"I need to, ah…" Conrad held up a finger and ran across the room in the direction of the restroom.

"What are we looking at here?" Sean asked the medic.

"It's too soon to know. The only thing I can say so far is that no one has demonstrated any life-threatening symptoms. Any idea what it might have been?"

Sean suspected the medic was holding back and giving him the sugarcoated version, but he was going to take it. "No idea. Just that it was probably put in the cake's icing."

"It wouldn't be something that would alter the flavor, then."

"Any ideas?"

"It could be a toxic plant. People wouldn't necessarily have noticed it. That means something that wasn't bitter or didn't produce an instant reaction. Some poisonous plants, such as elephant's ear, castor bean, and poinsettia, for example, can cause a burning sensation in the mouth."

Listening to the medic, it was clear he was knowledgeable on the subject. "How do you know all this?"

"My minor was herbalism during college."

"Do you think we're looking at a natural toxin, then, not something medicinal?"

"That would be my guess."

"Any specific plant you might suspect?"

"Aloe vera, foxglove, doll's-eyes… Just a start. My bet would be on the latter though, scientific name is actaea pachypoda, also known as baneberry. Aloe vera would have milder effects unless a person was allergic to it. Foxglove is more fatal, and we'd be seeing irregular heartbeat, mental confusion too. Some I've seen so far have exhibited a bit of delirium, but nothing acute. The berries of a baneberry plant have a bitter taste, of which no one has complained, so it's likely the plant stalk was used. Again, assuming it was baneberry. Good news it wasn't the berries too, as they are far more poisonous."

"How does baneberry poisoning manifest?"

"Pretty much as what you're seeing. Cramps, vomiting, and mild delirium. These symptoms are far worse in children, but it doesn't seem there are any here."

Sean shook his head. It was a no-children wedding.

The medic's face shadowed as he added, "Cardiac arrest is possible with baneberry poisoning, but only in extremely rare cases, and the dose would need to be very high. Same for ill effects to the nervous system."

Sean thought back to his friend's pale complexion, his perspiring brow, and his need to vomit. "So it can be fatal." Sean chewed on that.

"As I said, only in *extremely* rare cases."

The slim odds didn't make Sean feel any better. Everyone here was someone that he or Sara knew and loved. And Conrad specifically had eaten three pieces!

"And I mean *extremely* rare," the medic repeated yet again.

Sean nodded. "This baneberry lives in North America?"

"Mostly eastern North America, but the plant is dormant over the winter. It's a perennial, so the roots are there, and the plant will come up in the spring. If someone is just starting them, it's best to do this inside during the winter, then plant them in the early spring after the last frost. Given that we're just coming out of winter, assuming someone put it in the icing, they may have it in a greenhouse."

Sean nodded. The person who tampered with the cake may have been someone looking to start a garden for this coming season. "Can it be treated, and any adverse effects be reversed?"

"There are treatments available, yes. Usually, the symptoms present for about three hours, depending on dosage, obviously. But we'd need determine baneberry is what we're dealing with before any medical measures would be taken."

"Then what do you suggest?"

"Everyone affected needs to go the hospital and be monitored, tests run."

"Then let's get them there immediately." Sean thanked the medic, who then left to consult with his colleagues.

Conrad returned, a bit more color to his face than when he'd left.

"Feeling any better?" Sean asked him.

"Somewhat, but far from being right as rain."

Sean told him he'd have to be taken to the hospital and have tests run.

"Well, this day has taken quite the turns."

"That it has." Sean left Conrad to see to Sara, who was with her parents and her maids of honor. He was relieved to see that none of them looked anywhere near as bad off as Conrad.

He updated them on where things stood—how everyone would soon be ferried off to the hospital.

"At least I only had a small piece," Valerie said.

The others added their agreement.

Sara was fighting back tears, but a few fell when she hugged her parents and her friends.

Those who had eaten cake were herded toward the doors, and with Sara by his side, Sean informed Ryan and Louise of the situation.

"The medic I spoke with believes it could have been a toxic plant known as baneberry," he said.

"I'm familiar with that plant," Louise said. "It has little red berries, though some have white ones."

"I'll need to take your word on it," Sean said.

"If it's a plant in this climate," Ryan began, "is it alive all year?"

"Only if someone has it growing in a greenhouse. Seeds can be started inside during the winter months and planted in the ground come spring, after the last frost." As Sean prattled all this off, he was impressed by how much of what the medic had said stuck with him.

"If it was baneberry, then, the person who put it in the icing could be someone getting ready for summer season," Sara pitched in.

"Exactly what I thought," Sean agreed.

"Like you said, *if* it's baneberry," Ryan put in. "They don't know; that's why people are going to be tested."

"That's right." Sean appreciated the need to approach this situation with balanced expectations.

"Ryan, we should let everyone who isn't going to the hospital go home now," Sara said. "I'm sure you and the other officers have spoken to everyone by now, but I can get you a guest list."

Ryan shook his head. "Unless, people are going to the hospital, they stay put."

"You're being ridiculous at this point. Come on," Sara pleaded.

"Fine, everyone can go," Ryan eventually conceded. "Except us, the uniforms, the guards, and the investigators." He gestured toward two that entered the ballroom before going over to join them. Louise followed.

Sara turned to Sean. "That's something at least."

"This night goes from worse to even worse," he said.

"Night? Isn't it a new day by now?"

"If it's not, it will be soon. What do you say we go home and try to get some sleep?"

"Ryan just said we have to stay."

"He has no grounds to hold us here. We're not prisoners, Sara."

"I don't even know if I could get any sleep. My parents, our friends, so many of them are not well. If only Ryan had let them leave earlier, we wouldn't have brought out the cake and everyone would be okay." She palmed her cheeks, and Sean pulled her in for a tight hug. If he had his way, he'd never let go.

Chapter Twenty-Eight

Sara couldn't believe how a day that had started off with so much promise had become one nightmare after the next. Her mother looked terrified before she and Sara's dad were carted to the hospital. Even her father's eyes held fear, but he was putting on a brave front, being strong for Jeannie. Sara's friends were afraid too. How Sara would have given anything to remove all their apprehension and discomfort. The only thing that soothed her was believing that they'd all be fine, and that whatever had been added to the icing wasn't going to cause any serious damage or kill anyone. Still, who would have such a hateful heart to inflict this upon innocent people? If it was Mercer after revenge, why not do something targeted more directly at Sean and/or her? What would he gain from poisoning their guests? Surely, for Mercer to show up after all these years, he'd want more than to cause a disruption at their reception. Just the fact that he'd gone to the trouble of getting Hale out of the way so he could take his post with the security team told her that much. There had to be more to this that none of them were seeing yet.

Sean smiled kindly at her. "Let's go, then, if Ryan will let us."

"Sara?" Trinity was coming over to them with Austin at her heels.

"What is it?" Sara was happy to see the couple, as she had more questions for them, but she was a bit surprised. "Neither of you had any cake?"

They both shook their heads.

"The police said that I can't go home, but I don't know where I'm to go." Trinity sniffled and lowered to pet Magnum.

"That is procedure. Until it's understood exactly what happened to your aunt, her house will be off-limits," Sara laid out calmly. "Investigators will be searching it for any possible evidence that might lead them to her killer. You could stay at a hotel or with Austin."

"Killer," Trinity said, as if chewing on the word, and stood straight.

Magnum let out a low whine at the absence of affection.

Sara wriggled her fingers toward Magnum, and he sat down and quieted. *He obeys when it suits* him!

Trinity went on. "I can't believe this is happening, has happened. I heard rumors that some guy is coming after you and Sean. Did Aunt Dar interfere and wind up dead because of it?"

Sara looked at Sean. If he was thinking what she was, it certainly didn't take long for the rumor mill to gain traction.

"Did we hear correctly?" Austin asked, angling his head.

"It is possible there's someone here after me," Sean said. "But your aunt's murder—Sara and I believe—is a separate incident."

"But your guests were affected. What's to say this man with a vendetta against you two isn't why my aunt Dar is dead?" Trinity collapsed into herself, and Austin rubbed her back.

Sean looked away when Sara tried to make eye contact, but she could tell from his energy and the way his shoulders sagged he was taking the young woman's words too deeply to heart.

The girl wanted something, someone, to blame for her aunt's death, but Sara wasn't going to let Sean assume that burden. "We are not the ones who hurt your aunt, Trinity," Sara said firmly. "I admired her greatly. That's why I hired her to make our cake."

"But if she wasn't here, she'd still be…" Trinity left the rest unsaid and slid her bottom lip through her teeth.

"Possibly. But there's also a good chance her killer would have caught up with her another time." Sara was trying to read Trinity's energy and body language but was having a tough time doing so. Was this conversation about assigning blame, or to make a performance of her grief? Was her sorrow and indignation even genuine?

"Who, though? I mean who would want to do this?" Trinity ran a hand over her chin, wiping away some tears that had traced all the way down her cheeks.

Sara took a few deep breaths, wanting to ensure that what she'd say next would be stripped of all judgment. "We are trying to figure that out. Say, by chance, you don't own a beige purse?" That described the one they'd found in the coatroom with the feathers.

"Ick. Ah, no." Any trace of sadness was instantly wiped off her expression. "Beige? How boring, but no, I don't use purses, just this." She held out her hand to Austin, and he placed a cell phone in her palm. She opened the holder it was in. "It has slots for all my cards."

"What about cash?" Sean asked.

Trinity regarded him like he was a dinosaur. "Plastic's the now and the future."

"Speaking of the future, Trinity," Sara began. "We heard that you and Austin plan to get married." She phrased it as if it were a given.

"We wanted to, but Aunt Dar—" Trinity stopped talking and looked at Austin. "I guess there's nothing standing in our way now."

Sean hooked his eyebrows and glanced at Sara, and chills laced through her. They'd heard from Gertie about their loud argument on the topic, but Trinity's statement hit with weight.

"Your aunt didn't agree with the engagement?" he said, though it wasn't a fishing expedition, as he and Sara already knew the answer.

Trinity shook her head. "Nope. She thinks—or *thought*—I was too young for such a commitment."

"It would be a lot to balance with going to Juilliard," Sara inserted.

"She wasn't letting me go, so what did that matter? I swear sometimes she just wanted me to be unhappy."

Sara recoiled at that comment and said softly, "I guess you don't need to worry about that anymore either."

"Oh." Trinity's lips pouted. "I will miss her terribly. And maybe that was her job as my guardian to make sure that I thought things through, but her stubbornness was so frustrating at times. It felt like she was holding me back to spite me."

"She would have just wanted the best for you," Sara offered, believing every word.

Sean turned to Austin. "How did you feel about her aunt being against the engagement?"

"I half expected it." He scratched the back of his neck and seemed to be avoiding looking at Trinity.

Just that little slight, and Sara had a hunch he wasn't as sold on getting married anymore but hadn't yet broken that to Trinity.

"I'm sure you think I had a lot to gain from Aunt Dar's death." Trinity danced her gaze back and forth between her and Sean. "But I *lost* far more. She was my only living blood relative. Without her in this world, I have no idea where I belong, who I am." Her chin quivered, and her eyes pooled with tears.

Austin flinched at her remark, apparently still caring deeply for Trinity. He put a reassuring arm around her. "Let's just go back to my place tonight."

"You mean your parents' place? They'll never leave me alone long enough to get any sleep, and we'll be forced to rehash everything. I'm already exhausted."

"Okay, we'll get a hotel room for tonight."

The two of them walked off after Sara and Sean passed on their condolences.

Did she think Trinity was behind Darlene's death? Sara's gut told her otherwise. But it was nearing midnight, and she wasn't sure much was making sense to her anymore. She could barely keep herself upright. Between Darlene's murder, the tainted icing, and the sick friends and family, she just wanted to go to sleep and wake up to a fresh start. Hopefully sunrise would bring a better day. But it wasn't far from mind that Mercer was likely hanging around somewhere, intent on revenge. "I'm just burned out from this day."

"You and me both."

Magnum whined and paced at her feet.

"He must need out," Sara said.

"I say we leave and call it a night."

"We'll speak with the guards at the front on the way out, see if they can give us a description of the woman who impersonated Darlene and authorized Ralph Patrick's admission."

"All right, but then—" A huge yawn overtook her face. "Yep. Bed? I get it."

They left the ballroom with Magnum and told Ryan and Louise they were going to talk with the guards and then head home. He didn't object, and they didn't argue.

Sara imagined crawling into bed and tucking under the covers.

Chapter Twenty-Nine

Sara and Sean grabbed their coats before heading to the front doors. The plan was to speak with the guards and then leave. They found them standing inside.

"Mr. McKinley, sir, is there something we can do for you?" the bigger one asked, his gaze barely dipping to acknowledge Magnum. "Ma'am," he said to Sara.

They got their names—Garrett Golden and Doug Sanders.

"We understand that you admitted someone who wasn't on the guest list," Sean said.

That the invitation was fake was beside the point.

"That's right. We told Mr. Voigt that Darlene Day had cleared him." Garrett again, the apparent spokesman for the pair.

"What did she look like?" Sara asked.

Both security guards paled. "You don't know who she is, ma'am?" Doug asked.

"We know who Darlene Day is," Sara affirmed, "but we're quite certain that she wasn't the woman who told you to permit entry to Mr. Ralph Patrick."

"If you'd oblige us with a description." Sean gestured for them to do just that.

"Ah, sure, she was in her forties, possibly late thirties, wouldn't you say, Doug?" Garrett asked his partner.

"Yep. Brown hair, long, I'd say, but it was tied back in an up-do."

An up-do... It had been a while since Sara heard it put like that, but regardless, these attributes couldn't define the real Darlene Day by any stretch of the imagination. Darlene often had her hair gathered in a bun to prevent contaminating her baking. Otherwise, she was in her mid-sixties with gray hair. Unfortunately, the vanilla description of this mystery woman wouldn't get her and Sean far. "Anything else? An accent, jewelry she might have been wearing... Can you describe her dress?" That might be all Sara would need. Her memory was solid, and when it came to fashion, it was even more on point.

"She wasn't wearing a dress," Doug said.

"What was she wearing?" Sean asked.

"Pants paired with a collared shirt. All white."

That described the uniform the staff from Belle Catering wore. "Shoes?"

"Black and laced, flat or little heel," Doug said.

Goose bumps rose on Sara's arms. Practical footwear, and that matched what Trinity had told them about the person headed toward the kitchen as she was leaving. If the woman who approved Ralph Patrick's entrance was with Belle Catering, she most likely would have put her coat and purse in the coatroom adjacent to the kitchens. But where was this woman now? Surely, she'd be looking for her purse. Though how could she risk raising concerns about it? Much better to lose the purse and what was inside than to fall under suspicion of murder.

"Where was she when she gave this approval? Standing around or walking past?" Sean asked.

Sara thought that was a good question. At that time of day, the guards would have been posted outside.

"She was outside vaping," Garrett said.

It sounded as if this woman had been biding her time until Ralph Patrick's arrival.

"Why did you take her word for it that Ralph Patrick should be admitted? Why not check in with me, Sara, or Jimmy?" Sean asked, annoyance painting his tone.

"She told us she was close friends with you and that we could trust her," Doug said.

Sara bristled at that comment, but why should dishonesty surprise her? As she'd thought earlier, killers are conniving.

"Huh." Sean reached for Sara's hand. "Let's go."

Sara didn't hesitate, transferring Magnum's leash to the other hand so she could take Sean's. Stepping outside, the chill in the air seeped into Sara's bones, and she longed for a warm drink and her cozy bed.

The parking lot was quite dark, the two light posts not doing much more than casting a meager glow. Shadows edged in like hands reaching out to grab them.

"We have so much to think about here." Sean didn't sound as if he were even a touch leery due to the darkness. It wasn't far from her mind that Joe Mercer could be out there somewhere, watching them. Sean continued. "It would seem this woman was with Belle Catering, but who? And was she the one who tampered with the icing and killed Darlene?"

"I need to step back for a minute, Sean. Try to process everything. My head already hurts."

"Of course. I understand, sweetheart."

They reached Sara's Volkswagen Bug, and Magnum came to a full stop, lifted his nose in the air, and sniffed wildly. Then unexpectedly, he tugged on the leash, and Sara let go of Sean's hand to get a better hold on it.

"Something has him wound up," she said.

"I'll come pick him up and put him in the car." Sean started toward Magnum, who lowered to the ground and shimmied under the trunk.

Sara held up a hand to stay Sean. "Hold that thought…" They'd seen Magnum in action a few times now, and the dog had certainly proved he was gifted with the ability to sniff out trouble. Chills spread down her arms, and she looked around, feeling like the darkness had eyes. "Is there something under there?"

"I'll take a look." Sean hunched down and angled his head to peer at the undercarriage of the car. He quickly struggled to get back to his feet and scooped up Magnum. "Get away from the car now!" he yelled at her.

"Stop right there." Joe Mercer stepped out of the shadows.

Sara nestled into Sean's side. Magnum barked.

Mercer held something in his hands—not a gun but a palm-size device. "I'm guessing you found my little surprise."

The pieces clicked together for Sara. Sean's urgent rush to clear the area and what Mercer was holding. Magnum had sniffed out a bomb. The device in Mercer's palm was the detonator. Once again, the beagle had saved their lives—or at least prolonged them.

Sean stepped toward Mercer.

"Nah, nah, nah. I wouldn't if I were you." He held up the device. "All it would take is one little press of my finger, and you'd go *kaboom*."

Sara resisted the urge to point out that if he did so right now, he'd also die. She wasn't making the mistake of assuming he wasn't willing to be a martyr. Gratefully, if the bomb did go off—depending on how big it was—collateral damage would likely be minimal. The closest houses were a few lots to each side of the community center, and most of the parking lot had emptied out with the guests being permitted to leave. "Please, don't," she pleaded. "I'm sure we can talk this out like reasonable people."

"Ah, Mrs. McKinley, or should I say *Miss* Cain, as the nuptials never took place."

She recoiled at the obvious pleasure evidenced by his wild grin. It both hurt and angered her simultaneously.

Magnum picked up barking again, carrying on in a constant stream. It had Mercer moving back.

"Get him to shut up," he hissed. He was looking around, his shoulders hunched, no doubt concerned about the noise drawing attention.

Where are the cops who used to be outside? Had Mercer hurt them? In her head, Sara also kept screaming, *Louder, Magnum, louder!*

"I mean it," Mercer hissed as he pulled a gun from his jacket pocket and pointed it at Magnum.

Time slowed right down, and Sara saw all the dreams she had for a bright future with Sean and the beagle going up in smoke.

Chapter Thirty

Time was of the essence. It always was, which was
something Jimmy recognized the closer he got to
sixty. After turning fifty, he felt retirement stalking him,
and he didn't like it one bit. After all, what would he do
without the Albany PD in his life?

Sean had texted him about the situation at the venue
and that it was suspected someone had tampered with
the icing. Jimmy intended to do all he could to get some
answers.

Given Joe Mercer's apparent vendetta, it couldn't be
ignored that he might have put something in the icing.
He had substituted Hale's antibiotics with sleeping pills,
so he'd already proven what lengths he'd go to for his
cause. And poisoning the wedding guests would be a way
of making Sean watch on helplessly. It could fit, because
it would seem Mercer held Sean responsible for his
cousin's suicide—a situation that would have had Mercer
feeling powerless.

Jimmy hustled through the twenty-four-hour
pharmacy to the counter at the back of the store. Just
because Mercer had given Hale an over-the-counter
sleeping aid, it didn't remove the possibility he might

have used prescribed medicine to taint the icing. He flashed his badge to the pharmacist. "Sergeant Voigt. I have some questions about Joe Mercer."

The man seemed slow to respond—tiredness, discomfort at talking to a cop? It was hard to say why.

"Your name, sir?" Jimmy asked him.

"Phil Garrison. What's this about Joe?"

Jimmy looked around, though it was hardly necessary. The place was a ghost town at this hour. "I can't disclose that at this time, but I need to ask if you've noticed any missing inventory."

"You mean missing medication?"

"That's exactly what I mean." Jimmy had thought that was rather straightforward given the context—where he was and who he was asking.

"All our inventory is accounted for."

"So there's no way that any medication could have gone missing without your knowledge?"

"Between the pharmacist on the day shift and me, it's our job to review reports and physical inventory before we start work."

"And you did this at what time today?"

"Eight this evening, and as I said, the numbers showed no deficiencies."

It would seem, then, if Mercer was responsible for the tainted icing, it hadn't been with controlled medication. Had he used something off the shelf as he had done with Hale? There was something else that didn't align, though. "You said the numbers were in line—even the amoxicillin?" Jimmy raised his eyebrows. By all accounts, the pharmacist should show more in stock than the system showed sold.

"There was— You asked about shortages. How did you know about the amoxicillin? There was an overage I was curious about. Is that why you're here? Why you said you needed to talk about Joe?"

"Yes and no. But while we're on the subject, it seems likely that Mr. Mercer ended up intercepting a prescription for amoxicillin and substituted it for sleeping meds."

"What?" Garrison spat, then clenched his jaw and shook his head. "He's done. I'll fire him myself."

"You're his boss?"

"Joe works flexible hours. Sometimes during the day, other times at night. But I do have the authority to let him go."

"And tonight? Was he scheduled to work?"

"He was to work an extra-long shift today. He started early afternoon but went home sick before I got in."

Mercer showed up just long enough to make the substitution to Hale's prescription and then took off. Just how had he known that Hale would need amoxicillin? Then Jimmy recalled that Hale said he regularly refilled his prescriptions at this point in the month. Had Mercer substituted more than one just to cover himself? "Were you over on any other medications?" Jimmy realized that the pharmacist had made the distinction to his initial question—and fair enough.

"There were a few, yes."

"Were any of these medications prescribed to a Zeke Hale of Albany by chance?"

The pharmacist met Jimmy's gaze, and he could read his indecision about whether providing such information would be crossing a line.

"It would help to know," Jimmy said when seconds ticked off without a reply.

"One minute." He clicked on the keyboard, and a few seconds later, he nodded.

It was confirmed. Mercer likely tampered with all of Hale's prescriptions to ensure he didn't make the venue for the security job.

"I'm to guess that Joe is in trouble with the police? For you to be here?"

"Seems he is, but there's not much more that I can say." Jimmy pressed his lips. Getting fired would be the least of Mercer's worries by the time this was all over. He thanked the pharmacist for his help and turned to leave the store. On his way, he passed through the aisle that held various sleeping aids. It had him thinking of Hale again and what Mercer had used to drug him. What if Mercer had taken something from the shelf to use in the icing? How could he go about finding that? Then he had one thought.

He pivoted back to Garrison. The man looked livelier than he had been before their little talk—cheeks flushed, lips pursed. Anger must have stirred him awake.

"Is there something else I could help you with?" Garrison asked him.

"Possibly. Is there any way to know if there's been any unusual purchases of over-the-counter meds?" Jimmy was really fishing here. He was certainly no doctor and didn't even know what might cause the symptoms the wedding guests were experiencing.

"Hmm. Could you be more specific?"

Jimmy couldn't, really, not without disclosing more than he was comfortable doing. And really, what's to say that whatever Mercer used came from here? And even if it did, it might not be necessary that he buy a lot of it. But with every passing minute, Jimmy felt a bit more of a failure, as if he were letting everyone down. If they didn't find out what the guests ingested, it would be far more difficult for them to be treated effectively. Heck, it was even possible that the side effects could be exacerbated. "There is a situation in which people may be in danger."

Garrison leaned forward, placing his elbows on the counter. "Tell me what they are experiencing."

"Nausea, cramping… From what I understand, that's the worse of it."

"Huh." Garrison straightened back up. "Unfortunately, there are several things that could cause that, including food poisoning. E. coli, say if these people ingested contaminated meat. Then there's salmonella… I mean, the possibilities really are endless. On top of that, there are many medications that could do this if too much was ingested."

Jimmy was afraid the man might give him a buffet of options. "Well, thank you for your help."

"Can't say how much I helped, but thanks for opening my eyes to Joe Mercer."

Jimmy bobbed his head and tapped the counter before turning to head out. He hated to be leaving as empty-handed as he'd arrived. But honestly, he should have known better at his age than to hinge so much on a wing and a prayer. There was evil in this world, and sometimes there was no way of understanding it.

Chapter Thirty-One

Sean refused to allow things to end this way—for him, for Sara, for Magnum. "Mercer, your issue is with me. No one else. Let Sara and the dog go."

"No way. You see, they are leverage. They will get you to do what I want."

"And what is that?"

"To die. Painfully."

Sean refused to let this man see his fear—though it wasn't so much for himself as it was for Sara. He couldn't even fathom being this close to her when she died and being powerless to do anything about it. "Did you know that I fought for your cousin's freedom? For his sentencing to be reduced?" *That I might have actually saved his life in a standoff with the police…* If Sean hadn't intercepted, Giles Cochran could have been shot that day at the convenience store. And after Cochran was apprehended, Sean had spent hours talking with Jimmy and even turned up at the district attorney's house to try to talk down the charges—all of it to no avail. Giles Cochran's clean record up until that point accounted for nothing, just as his dire circumstances that instigated the event didn't justify his actions. The DA explained his position with the fact the prosecutor's office couldn't be seen as weak or more crimes would be committed by people using their bad luck as an excuse.

"You obviously didn't fight hard enough," Mercer spat.

Sean had passed Magnum's leash to Sara and set him on the ground. He'd managed to quiet the beagle, though there was a rumble emanating from his throat.

Sean's phone started ringing in his pocket, and he flinched.

"Leave it," Mercer told him.

Sean held up his hands and edged closer to Mercer. "Whatever you say. Just let them go."

"I told you that I'm not going to do that."

Magnum started barking again, tugging at the leash in Sara's hand.

"Actually, Sara, hand him back over to me." Sean reached for the leash, and as he did, he had an idea. It would be risky but might be their only chance at walking away from this.

"I told you. Shut that mutt up."

"Let me have a minute here…" Sean took the leash, hunched down to Magnum. He unhooked the leash from the dog's harness. The beagle quieted, and Sean could sense Mercer had calmed as a result. But the situation was still quite volatile. He couldn't risk underestimating Mercer's desire to see his plan through. Was he willing to kill himself in the process, or risk Sara's or Magnum's lives? And what about the people who lived in the area? How big was this bomb?

"Not in the mood to talk. The three of you will get into your car and stay put—or else." Mercer waved the gun in one hand, the bomb detonator in the other. "I'll get to a safe distance and then… Well, soon it will all be over."

Mercer puffed out his chest, and Sean let him assume he was calling all the shots. Meanwhile, he was still hunched beside Magnum, considering the plan he'd concocted. It was incredibly risky, but there wasn't much other choice. They'd need to make a Hail Mary move if there was to be any chance of surviving this. He and Sara certainly weren't going to load into her car with a bomb strapped under the bumper and wait to be blown to bits. Did Mercer think they were crazy? Instead, Sean was counting on Magnum to pick up on his silent cues, on the transfer of energy, if nothing else. Sara seemed to sense something as she glanced down and made eye contact with him. Just a brief look, but Sean hoped she received his message to run.

In a quick movement, Sean tapped Magnum on his rear and yelled, "Go get 'im, boy!" and "Run!" to Sara.

Magnum lunged forward, running at full speed, and Mercer screamed and ran. But he wasn't fast enough. Magnum jumped on his back, and Mercer slammed to the pavement. His gun and the detonator fell from his hands.

A loud, deafening explosion pierced the night air. The fireball lit up the sky, and the heat was intense.

The concussion flung Sean forward, and he barely kept his legs under him to avoid spilling to the ground. He looked around for Sara, hoping and praying that she'd made it out of the blast radius before the bomb was triggered. He spotted her silhouette at the far edge of the property line. From the looks of it, she was unscathed.

Sean scanned the lot and the yard, but he couldn't see the beagle. *Where are you, little fella?*

Mercer was still laid out on the ground and moaning as he struggled to hoist himself onto his side. He may have been injured but was alive.

Sean grabbed the gun and tucked it behind his cummerbund before Mercer got any wild ideas. Then Sean took the time to assess the damage.

The bomb was thankfully targeted and small. It had just been powerful enough to set the car ablaze and rock the earth. Sara's VW Bug was toast, but not much was damaged beyond that.

The security guards and Detectives Doyle and Farmer came running around the front of the center. *Sure, now they come!*

Sirens wailed in the distance and were growing louder.

"It's Mercer!" Sean shouted toward the detectives, indicating his wounded form. When he saw them running toward Mercer, Sean hurried to Sara. He took her in his arms, and she collapsed against him, likely seeking comfort in him as he was in her. At least they were alive.

"Where's Magnum?" she asked him as she pulled back.

"That I don't know."

"He probably got spooked and ran off."

He nodded, not wanting to disclose his fear that the situation may be far worse than that. And as much as he'd first resisted the canine, Magnum had managed to squirm his way into Sean's heart. He sure hoped the little fella was all right wherever he was.

A couple of fire engines arrived with the fire chief's SUV and an ambulance.

This day had been surreal, but Sean didn't need anyone to pinch him for reality to sink in. If they had been in the car when that bomb had gone off, he, Sara, and Magnum wouldn't be here to tell the tale.

Chapter Thirty-Two

Sara had pegged Joe Mercer as a formidable opponent when staring him down outside, but under the lights of the Dutch Community Center, he had lost all power of intimidation. Joe was caught and defeated. His hair was pasted to his head with sweat, and he was hunched forward in the chair. Thankfully, Sean's epiphany to create a distraction had paid off and Mercer had made a targeted bomb.

Magnum had yet to turn up, and that hurt Sara's heart, but it was time for Joe Mercer to answer for what he had done—what still may be in motion. If he had tampered with the icing, she didn't want to give too much thought to what the future might hold for those affected. Sean had received a text from Jimmy, who didn't have any luck finding out what may have been used.

Two security guys were asked to wander the neighborhood in search of the beagle, which freed up her and Sean to be present for questioning Joe Mercer.

Ryan and Louise put Joe in the meeting room that was becoming all too familiar. There was no sign of Desiree Moore or Ralph Patrick, so they must have been released and sent on their way.

Joe kept gripping his stomach. He must have been injured when Magnum had knocked him to the ground.

"Tell us what you put in that cake," Ryan roared, not standing on diplomacy, but many of those affected were people he knew as well.

"In the cake? I didn't do anything to any cake." Joe rubbed his sweaty forehead and looked down at his wet hand.

"You planted a bomb on the McKinleys' car," Ryan countered.

The only thing that sounded remotely good about that was being labeled a McKinley.

"Where are they?" It was Jimmy, and his voice traveled through the closed door of the meeting room.

"In there," a man responded.

The door swung open, and Jimmy stood in the opening. "What happened? I was gone for less than two hours. The fire department's outside, more police units, and the smoke is bothering me something crazy." As if on cue, Jimmy hacked, held up a finger to let those in the room know he wasn't finished talking. He cleared his throat. "Your car, Sara, it's cream puffed."

She'd let Jimmy's description pass. *Cream puffed* wasn't the right word, but it was totaled. "And Magnum's missing," she added.

"Oy vey." Jimmy turned his gaze to Joe and walked over, towering over the man. "You hurt good people tonight, and I will make sure you pay for that."

Joe flailed his arms but quickly dropped them and doubled over. "I didn't put anything in the cake! I don't even know what you're talking about."

"No? Cramps, headaches, vomiting…" Jimmy drew back. "Something like you're experiencing now, if I were to guess." Jimmy looked at Sara, then let his gaze travel to the rest of them in the room. "I don't think he's good for tampering with the cake."

"Finally, someone who believes me." Joe let out a deep sigh.

Jimmy's eye twitched, and he snarled, "You almost killed two of my favorite people in the world, and the sweetest pup on the planet better be out there alive. Count yourself lucky you committed this crime outside of my jurisdiction, or you'd never see the light of day again."

Sara, Sean, and the two Cotton Spring Falls detectives sat in silence as Jimmy had Joe Mercer cowering. But Jimmy was onto something with Joe and the cake.

"You did eat some cake, didn't you?" Just the thought of him doing so made her angry. This man, who intended to kill them, had eaten their wedding cake. The nerve! However he felt, he deserved every bit of agony. And that sort of thinking was uncharacteristic of her, but blame the hour and lack of sleep—or the fact he tried to blow them up!

"I did. But someone tampered with it?" Joe's eyes widened, showing more of the whites of his eyes.

Not all criminals are exactly bright...

"Don't you worry about that," Ryan said coolly.

"You said I've got the symptoms..." Joe looked at Jimmy. "Is it serious?"

"Guess we'll find out," Jimmy said nonchalantly, and left the room with the words, "I'm going to look for Magnum."

Sara got up from the table too, and Sean followed. While Jimmy went through the front doors to outside, she stopped with Sean at the entrance to the ballroom.

She wrapped her arms around herself and found that her hands were shaking. Scratch that, her entire body was trembling. The adrenaline from what had transpired outside was washing away, leaving her with the dire reality of what could have been if not for Sean's quick thinking. And going back further than that, Magnum deserved credit for alerting them that something was wrong in the first place.

"You're quaking," Sean said, opening his arms, and she tucked against him.

"There's just so much going through my mind. My parents and our friends to start. I wish we knew what was in the icing."

"I'm sure the doctors at the hospital will figure out how best to treat everyone."

Sara pulled out her phone and texted her mother, informing Sean what she was doing.

> *How are you? Any better? What are the doctors saying?*

As she waited for a response, the passing time was painful.

"She's probably with the doctor now and can't—" Sean stopped talking when Sara's phone chimed.

She read the reply from her mother.

> *Doctors aren't too worried it's anything serious… though may be too soon to know.*

"Sara?" The door of the meeting room swung open again, and Louise was coming toward them.

Sara held her phone tight in her palm, as if by doing so it would bring her parents and loved ones closer to her and she'd be able to heal them somehow. "Yes? What is it?" She tamped her emotions down—her fears, her grief, her sadness.

"I thought you might like to have a look at this." Louise held up a cell phone. "This was Darlene Day's."

Sara hesitated to take the phone as if it were poison. Even though something on it could give them answers. While she wanted to know, at the same time, she struggled with keeping her emotions under control.

Sean held out a hand toward Louise, and she set the phone in his palm. "Did you find anything?" he asked.

"Nothing much that we could make sense of. Maybe you two will have better luck."

"But Ryan would know Darlene far better than I do." Add guilt to the list of unwanted emotions flushing through her right now. Maybe if she hadn't left Cotton Spring Falls, Darlene Day wouldn't be dead. But what an egotistical thought! Whoever had killed Darlene had felt stabbed in the back and gotten her revenge—just as Joe Mercer had longed for his.

"Honestly? He's not seeing anything here. You might." Louise shrugged, walked a few steps, and pivoted. "I almost forgot. The niece gave us the passcode." She shared what that was with them and ducked back into the room.

Sean set about unlocking Darlene's phone, and Sara huddled close to his side. He brought up the text messages.

"Nothing here looks out of whack," Sara said and prattled off a few of the contact names. "They're all from Cotton Spring Falls, salt-of-the-earth people."

"All right, well, let's take a deeper look." Sean opened a few of them, and they read a few messages.

"Nothing incriminating. But I wouldn't expect so with these women. Go to her spam and blocked text messages, Sean."

"There are quite a few."

"Let's not get too excited yet. Scroll slowly." Most of the messages were still bold text, unread, but there was one that was read. She indicated it and said, "Open that one, and let's see if there's a thread."

"Not sure if it works that way, but let's give it a go." Sean clicked on it.

Last week: *All I wanted was a chance, but now you've left me no choice!*

A few hours before that: *Why can't you see that I'd be good for your shop?*

"Huh, well, this doesn't sound like run-of-the-mill spam," Sara said. "And 'good for your shop'? That sounds like this person was interested in Locally Baked."

"Agreed. Why wouldn't this flag for Ryan?"

"Beats me." When she'd worked with Ryan, she thought he was a thorough detective. Maybe it was how she had wanted to see him because she'd grown up with him. Had she been blinded by affording him the benefit of the doubt? "What's the number, Sean?"

He told her as she tapped it into Google on her phone. She almost dropped it when the source came up. "It's registered to Belle Catering." Again, it sank in that someone they had let into their wedding was responsible for taking a life. The if-onlys started circulating in her head. *If only* they had been more diligent. *If only* things had worked out differently. *If only* they had eloped, and she'd let go of the big wedding… Her inhalation caught in her chest on that last one. She had made such a huge deal about them getting married when the time was right.

Was there such a thing, or was it nothing more than an illusion or a procrastination tactic?

"Was Darlene working in conjunction with the catering company?" he asked, breaking through her thoughts.

"Not that I'm aware of. I wouldn't understand why she would have been anyhow."

"There's one thing we can try to see if we can get ourselves more context." Sean returned to the main screen for text messaging and selected the menu. There, he picked Archived.

Sara leaned in closer to him, her chin touching his bicep. "What do we have here?"

He was smiling. "I'm surprised you don't know this."

"Not a time to rub anything in, Sean." She looked up at him.

"When you delete text messages, even conversations in one go, they wind up in the— Can you guess?" He raised his brows at her, making a game of this.

"The Archived folder?"

"Ding, ding… Tell her what she's won."

"You're a goof." She smiled and shook her head at his nonsense, but she also appreciated the silly banter. It helped settle her nerves some. "Ah, Sean, that's the number right there." She pointed to the screen, and Sean opened that thread.

They scrolled to the beginning and worked down. The first text from this number was received two months ago.

Nice chat today. Great to meet a fellow baker.

You too.

"Darlene seems like a person of many words here," Sean said.

"Which is completely unlike her, but I can't see that she'd be that huge into texting. She'd prefer conversations that take place face to face."

"I can imagine that."

They resumed reading. The next message was from the anonymous person again and came in at the start of last week.

Why won't you just consider my proposal?

I'm not interested.

You may come to regret that decision.

You don't have any real experience. And don't you have a job?

Let me prove myself.

NOT HAPPENING!

Please.

Blocking your number!

And that was the last response from Darlene.

"Huh." Sean turned to Sara, and her mind was dissecting what they'd just read and drawing comparisons to what they knew.

"'Don't you have a job?'" Sara ruminated. "So this person must be an employee of Belle Catering, not the owner."

"I concur."

Sara let out a deep breath. Emma Belle was one of the nicest people Sara had ever met. She couldn't see her as a cold-blooded killer, and the description the guards gave them of the mystery woman didn't match either. "It would seem there is a conversation we're missing that took place in person or over the phone. But the sender wanted to—what?—work for Darlene? Take over her business?"

"I'm with what you said a moment ago. I think this person wanted to buy Darlene's shop."

"Yet you'd think that rumor would have come to us at some point today."

"True enough, the way word travels."

"Yep."

"We might need to wait until morning to find out who from Belle Catering was assigned this phone number."

"Can we really afford to wait, Sean? So many of our guests are affected by some unknown ingredient in the icing— Oh, I think some pieces are starting to click together. We asked before who might have wanted to hurt Darlene's business? We can't ignore the threatening tone to these messages: 'You may come to regret that decision' and 'Now you've left me no choice.'"

"Instead of hurting the business, maybe it was to put her *out of* business? A case of 'I can't have your shop, so no one can'? Make it so that the Bakery Box wouldn't be interested in purchasing either. Does Belle Catering specialize in baked goods?"

"Nope." She sighed. Just as it seemed they were getting closer to assembling the puzzle, all the pieces weren't yet fitting together.

"Seems like further proof they have nothing to do with her murder. Not the company anyway, but one of their employees." Sean met her gaze, and as he did, one name clicked into her head.

"Vanessa Brady. Sean, it must be her. She's new to town, she was here working for Belle Catering tonight. The timing of the first text is about right for when she arrived in town. Also, when new people come to town Darlene, my mother, and some others welcome them."

"That explains the 'nice to meet you' message."

"Uh-huh. She had also been wearing light pink lipstick. It had mostly worn off, but there was some here." Sara dabbed at the bottom of her lower lip. "It could have been a match to the tube in that purse we found."

"And feathers? You didn't happen to see any on her person, did you?"

"Nope. Now didn't you say that the paramedic thought baneberry was our culprit here?"

"That's right."

"And it could be started indoors, then moved outside in the spring?"

"Correct."

"Vanessa Brady would just be starting a garden this spring, Sean. She wasn't around for a previous spring or summer."

"If it is this baneberry, then she could have it in her house. She also could fit the description of the mystery woman the guards told us about."

"It's time to have a talk with Vanessa Brady."

"I'm thinking that sounds like a good idea."

The front doors opened, and Jimmy came inside with Magnum walking off-leash by his side. His little body wriggled as he hurried to close the distance to Sara and Sean.

She petted him and rubbed his soft, velvet ears. "So happy you're okay, little buddy."

"Me too." Sean lowered next to her to get in his fair share of cuddles.

They couldn't linger for long, though. If they were right, Vanessa was their best lead for getting a remedy for what ailed their guests at the hospital. She could confirm if it was baneberry or something else.

Sara stood. "Jimmy, we need a ride."

"Name the place, and I'll take you."

Sara told him they needed to go to the hospital, that Vanessa had gone along with the paramedics. And a few seconds later, they were on the move.

Chapter Thirty-Three

The fact that Vanessa Brady had left with the others to go to the hospital didn't prove her innocence to Sara. In hindsight, she'd deliberately licked the icing off her finger. And what better way to appear guileless than to play victim?

"Vanessa Brady, you said?" The nurse at the main desk in the hospital looked up at Sara.

"That's right." She was here with Sean; Jimmy had remained in the car with Magnum.

"I don't see that anyone by that name is currently being treated."

"But she was here?" Sara had this tingling sensation that Vanessa had simply used the chaos to make her escape.

The nurse shook her head. "Not that I'm seeing."

"All right. Thank you." Sara offered the woman a small smile, though the expression was forced. It weighed on her that in other rooms, in this very hospital, her family and friends were being treated due to some mysterious cause. "She saw a way out," Sara mumbled.

"Seem so," Sean agreed. "My question is, without her purse, how far could she get? She wouldn't even have keys for her house."

"I don't even want to give this much thought, but what if she wasn't planning to go home? She could have intended to skip town. Vanessa could have a phone holder like Trinity's and carry around all her credit cards and ID in it."

"Then Vanessa Brady could be anywhere, but we should stop by her house. At least rule it out."

She was torn. A part of her wanted to check on the wedding guests, but time could be put to better use finding out what the cake was tainted with. "Sounds like the next logical step to me."

They got on the road and were at the address listed for Vanessa Brady within fifteen minutes. Still, it felt like too long.

It was a two-story century-old house. There was a light on in the upper level.

"Someone's home," Sean said and pointed.

The four of them got out of the car, including Magnum.

"Okay, there's no reason to go into this situation blazing. Let's just breathe and approach this as if we're checking up on her welfare." She put that out there, her words far more calm and logical than her racing heart should support.

No doorbell, but Sean knocked loudly, and it carried through the early-morning air.

Inside the house, all seemed quiet.

"Someone's looking out." Jimmy was standing back from the porch with Magnum and pointed at the second story. "Can't tell if it's a woman or not."

"As far as I know, Vanessa is single," Sara said.

Sean knocked again, and this time, there was movement inside the house that vibrated the porch floorboards beneath their feet. A few seconds later, the door opened.

Vanessa was standing there. Her hair that had been pulled back and tidy earlier was now frizzy around her face, and some strands had broken loose and were dangling to her shoulders. "Sara?" Her gaze traveled past Sara to Jimmy and Magnum. "What is everyone doing here?"

"We just wanted to check in and see how you're feeling." Sara was disgusted by Vanessa's deceit, but she was a killer, so why should Sara be surprised by her lack of morals?

"Just fine actually. Guess I was lucky." She tucked a wild strand of hair behind her ear.

"Good to hear that. Could we come in for a minute?"

"Ah, sure." Vanessa stepped back and opened the door wider for them.

Her hospitality did little to curb Sara's suspicions. If anything, it strengthened them. A person with something to hide could feel the need to overcompensate with kindness. Sara had a hunch that was the case here.

"Beautiful home." Sara made a show of looking around. High ceilings, and original architectural touches remained in the staircase railing, balusters, and hardwood floors.

"It is," Sean pitched in.

Magnum's nose was high in the air, sniffing wildly. He stepped toward Vanessa. She stepped back.

"Anyone want something to drink? I don't have much. Water, tea, coffee? It's no trouble."

"We're fine. Thank you," Sean said, responding on everyone's behalf.

Vanessa kept looking at Magnum, anxious.

"Don't like dogs?" Sara asked nonchalantly.

"I had a bad experience with one when I was younger. I'm more of a cat person." Vanessa rubbed her arms. "I don't mean to come across as rude, but what is it that I can do for you? It is one thirty in the morning."

Cat person, Sara believed, but she didn't think Vanessa was being fully truthful. She was being cagey. "We just have some questions for you." She put it out there as if Vanessa could help them, not that she was suspected of any wrongdoing.

"Whatever you need." She gestured to Sara to go ahead.

And there it was again—overcompensation. She probably thought that by being cooperative, she was communicating innocence when, in fact, it was the exact opposite.

Vanessa took another step away and directed them to a living room off the entry. "Make yourselves comfortable. Even you," she added, pressing on a smile for Magnum.

The beagle was restless, his nose still sniffing the air. It might not mean anything, though, considering Vanessa's home was new territory. It would be full of new and as-of-yet-unexplored scents, but Sara had a hunch the beagle was onto something specific.

Sara, Sean, and Jimmy unzipped their coats and sat around the living room.

"We won't be too long. As you said, it is early." Sara smiled pleasantly, but as she had undone her zipper, she felt a subtle draft dance across the exposed flesh at her collar.

"What is it that you'd like to ask me?" Vanessa leaned forward, then back. She didn't seem to know what she wanted to do with her arms and hands. Her body language fluctuated between open and closed off.

"How well did you know Darlene Day?" Sara asked. They'd agreed on the way over that since Sara was from Cotton Spring Falls, she'd do the talking.

"Oh, Darlene." A flicker crossed her facial expression, but it was one Sara had a hard time reading. "It's just awful what happened to her."

"I agree, and all of us will do whatever we can to help the police apprehend her killer." That statement might have been a little bold, too much of a punch, but it was also a test. How would Vanessa react? As per the script the woman must have running in her head—the one of innocence—she puffed out a breath as if deeply grieved.

She clutched the collar of her shirt. "But I'm not sure how this affects you. You're not police anymore, from what your mother told me."

Vanessa still hadn't answered her question, and now she'd deflected. "Jimmy still works for the Albany PD. You seem to know that Sean and I used to, but seeing as Darlene was murdered at our wedding, we have a special interest in finding out who did this to her. How well did you know Darlene?" Sara intentionally spoke fast, leaping from one point to the next.

"I would have liked to have known her more, but I've only been in town a short time. She was part of the welcoming team that came here when I first arrived."

"It must have been nice to meet a fellow food enthusiast." It was too soon to put out *baker*.

Vanessa's eyes met Sara's. "Why would you assume that about me?"

"You work for Belle Catering, don't you? You must like food, working with food…"

"Ah, sure."

Sara could feel the woman's guard weaken when the conversation veered to a more personal subject. It was time to execute the next phase of the plan. "Could I use your bathroom?"

"Yes. It's down the hall, off the kitchen."

"Thanks." Sara got up, glancing at Sean and Jimmy. Both acknowledged her with brief eye contact.

She headed in the direction that Vanessa told her to go and kept going. There was a four-season room at the back of the house, and it was dotted with various plants. Sara didn't have a green thumb by any means, but she had looked up baneberry on the internet on the way over. She'd like to think she could identify it if she found it here.

Another draft caught her unprepared, and shivers laced her spine. She followed it and found its source was a broken window next to the back door. If Vanessa had been the owner of that purse, she wouldn't have her house or car keys. She'd have had to break into her home. From the looks of it, that was exactly what she did. And that told Sara all she needed to know. Vanessa Brady had killed Darlene Day.

"Can I help you?" It was Vanessa.

Sara must have been so caught up in her thoughts, she hadn't heard that the conversation in the living area had wrapped up. Even the older floorboards in the home did nothing to warn her of incoming company.

She spun around, a smile in place. "I'm so horrible with directions."

"You would have gone right past the bathroom." Vanessa flicked a finger toward the doorway that Sara had noted.

She shook her head as if she were losing her mind. "It is early—late—however you want to look at it."

"Yes, a long time without sleep." While Vanessa's words hinted at lightness, there was nothing light about her demeanor.

Sara excused herself and, once in the bathroom, she texted Sean.

She broke in. Bit of a greenhouse going. Didn't spot baneberry. Doesn't mean it's not here. Try the number we have.

The message was quickly marked as read, and Sara went through the motions of making it sound like she'd finished her business. She flushed the toilet and washed her hands.

When she stepped out, Vanessa was standing in the doorway, arms crossed. "I didn't want you to lose your way back to us."

"How thoughtful. You go ahead, and I'll follow." No way was Sara going to walk in front of this woman, not after what she had done to Darlene.

"Sure." Vanessa led the way.

Sean had his phone to an ear when they walked back into the living room. He'd have called the number associated with Belle Catering that they'd found on Darlene's phone. A faint ringtone sounded from upstairs. This was the outcome Sara had expected, but it still sent chills through her to have her hunch confirmed.

Vanessa stiffened, and Sara went to move, but she wasn't fast enough. Vanessa got a hold on her and pulled her close. In her hand was a knife, and she held it to Sara's throat.

Just great!

Sean and Jimmy stood and came toward them. The ringing stopped, and Sean pocketed his phone.

"What are you doing?" Sara said to Vanessa.

"Like you need to ask," Vanessa hissed. Any pretense at being a concerned citizen was gone.

"Why did you kill Darlene?" This was the second time Sara had faced death within the last two hours, and somehow, having survived the first time had emboldened her.

"I never said I did."

"Your actions aren't those of an innocent person," Sean said calmly, stepping closer.

"Stop there, or I will kill her."

Vanessa was shaking. While she might have killed Darlene, possibly even premeditated how it would play out, Sara didn't sense that Vanessa was comfortable about taking life. Could that work in her favor? "I'm guessing Darlene hurt your feelings. She could be like that…"

"Like what?" Vanessa's hand faltered just slightly.

"Thoughtless. She tended to speak her mind without a filter. She got on a lot of people's nerves." Sara was painting Darlene as some busybody who pushed people away. It couldn't have been further from the truth. If Darlene had decided against a friendship with Vanessa, it was because she could sense something was off with her. From what Sara was seeing, her intuition had been spot-on.

"It wasn't just me, then? She was so cruel to me, and I didn't do anything to her."

Sara, Sean, and Jimmy kept making eye contact, fleeting, communicative, hoping that Vanessa wouldn't pick up on it.

"She took a while to warm up to outsiders," Sara said, doing her best to be sympathetic.

"She shouldn't have been on the welcoming committee. Pah," Vanessa spat.

"I agree with you." Sara held up her hands.

"If you hated her so much, why did you hire her to do your cake?"

Think, Sara, think… "My mother made me do that."

"Nah, I don't believe you. You're just trying to get me to talk, to make me think you understand how I feel, but you have no idea."

"I know what it's like to be rejected." Sara pulled from deep inside for this admission, tugging at a scar that might never heal. But given her texts to Darlene, Sara pegged rejection at the root of Vanessa's motivation.

"How could you possibly know? You have a man who adores you."

Sara had struck it right. At the source of Vanessa's issues was a deep-set feeling of abandonment and rejection. It had started with her cheating husband, if not before. Then Darlene's turning her back on her hadn't just amplified the hurt but had become a catalyst for murder. "I have Sean, but I've never known my birth mother. She abandoned my father and me when I was a baby."

"Your sob story isn't working on me. Look at you now. You've turned out just fine. What do I have?" Tears were falling down Vanessa's cheeks.

Magnum barked, as if sensing a shift in energy. It was more unsettled and volatile with every passing second. Sara had to get that knife away from her throat if she wanted to stand any chance of coming out of this alive.

Sara said, "You have this beautiful house, a good job—"

"Whatever. I rent here. Not like I could get a mortgage with my credit—not after my husband destroyed it!" Vanessa hissed.

Magnum's barking was becoming more insistent, and he was straining at the leash in Jimmy's hand.

"Sorry to hear that you suffered all that," Sara said. "And I can understand why Darlene's cruelty on top of it may have pushed you over the edge. But why hurt everyone at the wedding? Why tamper with the icing?"

"You don't get anything, do you?" Vanessa pushed Sara away from her, an instinctual reaction, but it had Sara taking a breath of relief. She also took the opportunity to put more space between herself and Vanessa's knife.

"Tell us what we don't understand." This from Sean, interjected in the ear-piercing silence that followed Vanessa's statement. Even Magnum had quieted.

"I wanted to destroy her. Some big bakery wanted her shop, and she wouldn't give my offer the time of day. I would have kept it small and local, just as she wanted."

"Did you have experience running a bakery?" Sara wasn't even going to poke for the details of Vanessa's offer at this point, but it did pique her curiosity, considering she'd just said she had no credit.

"I had my own shop years ago, but Darlene said I was out of practice and not up to her standards." Vanessa was flailing the knife around in the air.

"What did you put in the icing?" Sara was frazzled and desperate for the answer.

"Nothing that's going to kill anyone, just cause some temporary discomfort."

"Some people got really sick," Sean said, and Sara knew he was referring to his friend Conrad Cooley.

"What was it?" Sara pushed.

"Baneberry. Very little."

Sean pulled out his phone, likely to contact the hospital to inform them their guests ingested baneberry. "I need to make a call."

"Makes two of us." Sara got on her phone and called Ryan to come get Vanessa Brady.

Vanessa looked at Sara. "I wasn't supposed to get caught."

"What was your end game, anyway?" Sara asked.

"Honestly? I never thought that far ahead, but I'd have loved to get away with murder."

"Not on their watch." Jimmy flicked a finger toward Sara and Sean and relieved Vanessa of her knife.

In the stillness that followed, Sara felt like she could collapse. Everything and everyone should be okay now. Well, except for poor Darlene, but at least there would be justice.

Chapter Thirty-Four

The Following Friday

Sara was being fussed at by her mother and two maids of honor in the restroom of the Albany courthouse. She and Sean had discussed taking the wedding abroad, going somewhere fun overseas and flying everyone out for the festivities, but Sean's aunt was terrified of flying. Two things that she and Sean agreed on were their big day couldn't wait any longer and they wanted their closest friends and family present when they exchanged vows. It had been the better part of a week since their planned wedding, but in some ways, it felt much longer than that.

Vanessa confessed to the murder and to adding baneberry to the icing—the latter of which crime scene investigators could support. She refused to get into the details of exactly how she had managed to pull that off, but it wasn't required to put her away for a good long time. There were some baneberry plants found in her home greenhouse. She had broken down during interrogation saying that she just couldn't take an old lady rejecting her after her husband had. It came out that her offer for Locally Baked involved a complicated lease-to-own arrangement, and Sara couldn't fault Darlene for not being interested.

But in the hours Detectives Doyle and Farmer had questioned her, Vanessa claimed she never intended to kill Darlene. She admitted to inviting Ralph Patrick to stir things up for Darlene, saying she wanted the man from the Bakery Box to have a front-row seat to Darlene's failure—the tainted icing.

Vanessa had gone into the kitchen to give Darlene one last chance to let her buy the bakery, but she turned her down. By that point, Darlene had eaten some cake and felt sick. She accused Vanessa of sabotaging the cake and was going to report her actions to Emma Belle and get her fired. Vanessa snapped and grabbed what was handy—a cake serving knife—and plunged it into Darlene's back when she'd turned around. Then Vanessa exited through the staff coatroom, into the second kitchen, and out into the dining room.

The purse that Magnum had sniffed out in the coatroom did belong to Vanessa, and the feather found under the counter must have gotten attached to Vanessa's person—her phone holder or slipped out of a pocket. That part wasn't clear, though Vanessa admitted to having a fascination with feathers—for a reason she couldn't explain—and collecting many she came across. As for the second cake serving knife, Belle Catering had brought it along.

And even though they had most of the answers, it failed to do one thing: bring Darlene Day back to life. It served as a dark cloud over what was to have been Sara and Sean's happy day, but justice was served in the end.

Trinity did inherit all that Darlene had and was going to keep the bakery and hire a manager to run the day-to-day while she applied to Juilliard for the coming fall. As for the mystery of who Darlene had been arguing with the night of the rehearsal dinner, it had turned out to be Trinity. She'd popped into the restaurant but ended up leaving with Austin. A benefit to all this coming out after Vanessa's arrest was it hadn't influenced the investigation and delayed its resolution.

Ryan and Louise had gotten further with Joe Mercer too. He blamed his favorite aunt's chronic alcoholism on Sean. She'd started drinking after her son, Giles Cochran, died by suicide. Her recent death from cirrhosis of the liver had stirred a need for revenge. He admitted to finding out how to build a bomb on the internet.

Gratefully, she and Sean weren't being brought up on any charges of interfering in a police investigation—a grace of God. Ryan, though not thrilled Sara and Sean confronted Vanessa without him and Louise, was letting it go.

"All right, well that's that." Jeannie stepped back from Sara and smiled at her daughter, tears beading in her eyes.

The moment incited déjà vu, and Sara was overcome with nerves—and excitement. The time had come to commit to the man she loved for the rest of her life.

"Let's do this." She smiled at her mother before moving in to kiss her cheek and get one in return.

Her mother and two best friends did a group hug and then filtered down the hall. Sean, his aunt, Conrad Cooley, Jimmy, and Magnum—a bow tie around his little furry neck—were all waiting.

Sara resisted the urge to cry and drew up alongside Sean.

"You ready?" he asked her.

"Past ready."

"And you're sure you want to do it this way... in a courthouse with a justice of the peace?"

"Sean, I just want to be your wife, and I don't want to wait another minute."

"I love to hear that."

The door opened, and a young woman poked her head into the hall. "Sean McKinley, Sara Cain?"

"This is it." Sean took her hand, and the group entered the room.

As she and Sean crossed the threshold, Sara knew this was just the beginning of something beautiful. Sean must have felt it too, as he looked over at her and winked.

Catch the next book in the Sara and Sean Cozy Mystery Series!

Sign up at the weblink listed below
to be notified when new Sara and Sean Cozy Mystery
titles are available for pre-order:

CarolynArnold.net/SSUpdates

By joining this newsletter, you will also receive exclusive
first looks at the following:

Updates pertaining to upcoming releases in the series,
such as cover reveals, book descriptions, and firm release
dates

Sneak peeks of teasers and special content

Receive insights that give you an inside look at Carolyn's
research and creative process

A Letter From Carolyn

Dear reader,

I want to say a huge thank you for choosing to read *Wedding Bells Brew Murder*. If you would like to hear about new releases in the Sara and Sean Cozy Mystery Series, be sure to sign up at the following link. Your email address will never be shared, and you can unsubscribe at any time.

CarolynArnold.net/SSUpdates

If you loved *Wedding Bells Brew Murder*, I would be incredibly grateful if you would write a brief, honest review.

For those of you familiar with the Albany, New York, area, you'll be wondering where I came up with Cotton Spring Falls. Well, my imagination! It's a completely fictional town that I created for this series.

Should you want to continue investigating murder, you'd be interested to know that I offer several international bestselling series for you to savor—everything from crime fiction to thrillers and action adventures.

I'd be remiss not to mention those who supported me with this project along the way. You know who they are—thank you! And my sweet husband, George, you continue to be my greatest asset.

Last but certainly not least, I love hearing from my readers! You can get in touch on my Facebook page, through Twitter, Goodreads, or my website. This is also a good way to stay notified of my new releases.

You can also reach out to me via email at Carolyn@ CarolynArnold.net.

Wishing you a thrill a word!
Carolyn Arnold

Connect with CAROLYN ARNOLD Online:
CarolynArnold.net
Facebook.com/AuthorCarolynArnold
Twitter.com/Carolyn_Arnold

CAROLYN ARNOLD is an international bestselling and award-winning author, as well as a speaker, teacher, and inspirational mentor. She has several continuing fiction series and has many published books. Her genre diversity offers readers police procedurals, hard-boiled and cozy mysteries, thrillers, and action adventures. Her crime fiction series have been praised by those in law enforcement as being accurate and entertaining. This led to her adopting the trademark: POLICE PROCEDURALS RESPECTED BY LAW ENFORCEMENT™.

Carolyn was born in a small town and enjoys spending time outdoors, but she also loves the lights of a big city. Grounded by her roots and lifted by her dreams, her overactive imagination insists that she tell her stories. Her intention is to touch the hearts of millions with her books, to entertain, inspire, and empower.

She currently lives near London, Ontario, Canada with her husband and two beagles.

CONNECT ONLINE
CarolynArnold.net
Facebook.com/AuthorCarolynArnold
Twitter.com/Carolyn_Arnold

And don't forget to sign up for her newsletter for up-to-date information on release and special offers at CarolynArnold.net/Newsletters.

9 781989 706923